Juliet rarely wore heels any more, but she knew they would give her some much-needed confidence today. At five feet two inches she needed all the help she could get in the height department, and a couple of extra inches immediately improved her self-assurance.

There was a large gust of air as someone pushed open the door, and the movement drew Juliet's attention. A stray shaft of sunlight illuminated a man as he entered the room—tall, smartly dressed and familiar.

It was Sam.

The love of her life. Her husband.

Soon to be her ex-husband.

But circumstances weren't enough to stop the tingle that surged through her every time she saw him. In her eyes he still looked as good as the day she'd met him.

He paused just inside the doorway, and Juliet took a moment to admire him. He was wearing his white naval officer's uniform, the crisp, clean colour even more eye-catching against the dirty, dull tones of the room. But then she'd always been a sucker for Sam in his dress uniform…

Dear Reader

This book is my fourth linked tale—I seem to be developing a habit! You might recognise my heroine Juliet from my last book, DR DROP-DEAD GORGEOUS. She was the heroine's sister, but she was having her own interesting experiences and was demanding that I tell her story too. I have never started a book knowing it's going to be the first in a series, but somewhere along the way my secondary characters develop to a point where I can't abandon them. So it was with Juliet.

She has had a rough eighteen months. A divorce, surgery and chemotherapy have taken their toll on her, and now she's a single mother to two young children and about to undergo more surgery. Juliet would love to turn the clock back a few years—wouldn't all thirty-something women?—but she knows that's impossible, and she's just hoping for a brighter future. I wanted Juliet to have that bright future. I wanted her to be happy. But the trouble was I'd already divorced her from the love of her life. Could I help her to find love a second time, or had her luck expired? Answering that question became my goal.

Juliet and Maggie are the second pair of sisters I've written about. That is no surprise to me, because I am lucky enough to share a close bond with all my siblings, including two sisters, and I enjoy giving life to characters who share that same relationship. It's a fabulous thing to have a person in your life who loves you unconditionally, and I hope that everyone reading this has someone—be it a sister, friend, daughter, cousin or mother—you know will catch you if you fall or who will let you catch them. This story is for all the women of the world.

Best wishes

Emily

NAVY OFFICER
TO FAMILY MAN

BY
EMILY FORBES

First published in Great Britain 2011
by Mills & Boon,
an imprint of Harlequin (UK) Limited,
Large Print edition 2011
Eton House, 18-24 Paradise Road,
Richmond, Surrey TW9 1SR

© Emily Forbes 2011

ISBN: 978 0 263 21749 0

Harlequin (UK) policy is to use papers that are
natural, renewable and recyclable products and made
from wood grown in sustainable forests. The logging
and manufacturing process conform to the legal
environmental regulations of the country of origin.

Printed and bound in Great Britain
by CPI Antony Rowe, Chippenham, Wiltshire

Emily Forbes began her writing life as a partnership between two sisters who are both passionate bibliophiles. As a team Emily had ten books published, and one of her proudest moments was when her tenth book was nominated for the 2010 Australian Romantic Book of the Year Award.

While Emily's love of writing remains as strong as ever, the demands of life with young families has recently made it difficult to work on stories together—but rather than give up her dream Emily now writes solo. The challenges may be different, but the reward of having a book published is still as sweet as ever.

Whether as a team or as an individual, Emily hopes to keep bringing stories to her readers. Her inspiration comes from everywhere: stories she hears while travelling, at mothers' lunches, in the media, and in her other career as a physiotherapist all get embellished with a large dose of imagination until they develop a life of their own.

If you would like to get in touch with Emily you can e-mail her at emilyforbes@internode.on.net and she can also be found blogging at the Mills & Boon® Medical™ Romance blog— www.eharlequin.com

Recent titles by the same author:

DR DROP-DEAD GORGEOUS
THE PLAYBOY FIREFIGHTER'S PROPOSAL
WEDDING AT PELICAN BEACH

This book is dedicated to two women without whom this book would still be just an idea in my head.

Thank you firstly to my sister, Belinda. We started our writing lives together, and having someone with whom I could plot and scheme, share ideas and solve problems, made the idea of writing a book seem possible. Together we achieved our dream. Our partnership gave me the confidence to go solo, but I know I could not have got to this point without you, and I look forward to reuniting our writing lives again one day.

In the same way that this book would never have begun without my sister, I can honestly say it would also never have been finished without the invaluable support and wise words of advice of my editor, Lucy. It's wonderful to work with someone who understands what I'm trying to achieve, and your precise, sanguine suggestions are always welcome.

I am thrilled to be able to dedicate this book to you both as my way of saying thank you!

CHAPTER ONE

JULIET entered the courthouse, passing through the security screening area and into the foyer. Her unfamiliar heels clicked on the marble floor, echoing in the space, as she strode towards the notice-board on the opposite side of the atrium. She rarely wore heels any more, not since she'd given up a career in law for a career as a university lecturer, but she knew adopting a power-dressing approach would give her some much-needed confidence today. She'd deliberately chosen one of her old suits—she'd barely worn it and hoped it still passed inspection—and she'd teamed it with the confidence-boosting heels. At five feet two inches she needed all the help she could get in the height department and a couple of extra inches immediately improved her self-assurance.

She checked the list of the day's cases pinned to the board, looking for her name and case number. She found it, about a third of the way down. Today she was nobody special, just another number. She headed for courtroom number three, making her way towards the waiting area.

The waiting annexe was sombre, dull and out-dated, depressing. Gone was the imposing decor of the entrance foyer, the marble floor and chandeliers giving way to stained carpets, fake wood wall-panelling and a mismatched collection of chairs, some plastic, some scratched timber and some with faded upholstery. She wasn't inclined to sit down.

Juliet knew she was being ridiculous with her silent criticism; the dull room was perfectly suited to her mood, but she wasn't used to feeling depressed and she wanted the room to lift her spirits, not contribute to the feeling of finality. She wanted the room to instil in her a sense that she was doing the right thing but all it was doing was making her feel worse. It exacerbated her loneliness and increased her sorrow.

But there was no turning back, despite her sister's parting words as she'd dropped her off at the courthouse earlier. Juliet had come this far and she wasn't changing her mind now. There had been times where she could have backed down, where she could have stopped this day from coming, but not now. Not any more. The decision had been made.

Juliet had always been stubborn and that hadn't changed. She sighed and chose a seat on the right-hand side of the room. While she sat waiting for her case number to be called she looked at the other people scattered around the room. Mostly they looked tired and worn out and their demeanour did nothing for her mood either. All of them were in everyday clothing, none of them had bothered to smarten up their attire, and the contrast between their outfits and hers flattened her confidence a little.

The weak winter sunlight struggled to penetrate the grimy windows, the glass surfaces were smeared with dirt, too high up to be easily cleaned and it looked as though no one had bothered for years. Juliet was watching the floating dust motes as they wafted through the sporadic beams of light, pushed about by the invisible breaths of air as people moved about the room. A large gust of air disturbed the dust as someone pushed open the door and the movement drew Juliet's attention. A stray shaft of sunlight illuminated a man as he entered the room, tall, smartly dressed and familiar.

It was Sam.

The love of her life. Her husband.

Soon to be her ex-husband.

But circumstances weren't enough to stop the tingle that surged through her every time she saw him. In her eyes he still looked as good as the day she'd met him.

He paused just inside the doorway and Juliet took a moment to admire him, knowing she didn't have long before he would find her in the small room. He was wearing his white naval officer's uniform, the crisp, clean colour even more eye-catching against the dirty, dull tones of the room. But, then, she'd always been a sucker for Sam in his dress uniform.

He was tanned from his time spent on the ocean and in the sun, his olive skin contrasting with the white fabric of his clothing. His thick blond hair was slightly longer than usual, long enough to be showing a little of its natural curl as it brushed the nape of his neck.

His eyes scanned the room and settled on her.

He moved towards her, smiling his crooked smile. She'd never been able to resist his smile. It started on the right side of his mouth, that corner always lifted first, before the smile spread across his lips, revealing a row of perfect, white teeth, until it reached the left corner, by which time Juliet always found she was smiling too. Even now his smile was working, lifting the sombre mood, lifting her spirits, if only temporarily.

In a few steps Sam had reached her side. He sat beside her on an upright wooden chair and leant across to kiss her cheek.

'How are you?' he asked. His voice sounded calm and controlled, completely the opposite to how she felt. She was apprehensive and nervous, plus she'd been unable to sleep soundly for several nights and now she was exhausted. But she told him none of this.

'Good,' was her reply. 'And you?' She sounded so polite, almost as though she was talking to a stranger, not to someone who had shared her bed for a third of her life.

Up close she could see that Sam had a few more wrinkles at the corners of his green eyes and a few strands of grey in his blond hair.

Neither detracted from his looks. He was still a handsome man and Juliet imagined he would always be. He would age well, she thought. She wondered how they looked to the other people in the room. What did they think she and Sam were there for? Would anyone guess they were about to get divorced? Would anyone else care?

'How long until it's our turn?' His voice interrupted her thoughts. If he had any trace of concern he was hiding it well, sounding relaxed and completely unfazed by the situation. She could imagine him in a crisis on board a naval vessel, directing sailors, getting people to do what he wanted without having to yell. Nothing much ever seemed to rattle him and it looked as though today was no exception.

'I'm not sure,' she answered. 'I think there are still a couple of cases before us.'

She felt Sam's arm brush against hers and the contact made her look down. He was pinching the crease in his trouser leg, a crease she could see was ironed to within a fraction of perfection. Juliet could see the outline of the muscles in Sam's thigh straining against the fabric. His leg was too close to hers, making her feel an unfamiliar sense of unease. He was too close. She wished he'd left a seat between them, kept some distance, then maybe she would have been able to calm her nerves.

Sam looked fit, healthy and full of life. A huge contrast to the rest of the crowd and probably a huge contrast to her. She felt tired, a feeling she was getting used to and had attributed to life as a single mother. Sam, on the other hand, looked as energetic as the day they'd met. Thirteen years ago.

She kept her gaze focussed on her lap. She didn't want to look at Sam, couldn't face seeing him there. All it did was remind her of everything she was losing.

How had they come to this?

Her sister Maggie had suggested that she could still stop this process but Juliet felt they'd tried everything they could and still they were in front of the magistrate. She'd tried, they both had, but in the end they'd run out of options. A marriage couldn't work without compromise.

Her hands were shaking. She grabbed her handbag from the chair beside her, pulling it onto her lap, holding it firmly in an attempt to stop the shaking. Her engagement ring caught the light, shooting sparks over the floor in front of her, small bright spots glistening in the dirt. She hadn't removed her rings as in her mind she was still married. For a little longer anyway. She sneaked a sideways glance at Sam's hands. He still wore his wedding ring too.

'How are the kids?' Despite Juliet's less than enthusiastic responses, Sam continued to attempt to make conversation and Juliet thought she'd better make an effort to hold up her end.

'Fine,' she answered honestly. 'They're doing fine.' It was true too, but, then, they were used to their father being absent for long periods of time. Even when he had lived with them he could spend months at sea. They thought it was normal.

Juliet hadn't wanted it to be their normal circumstances. She'd wanted them to have a father who was around. She and Sam had planned for that to happen but their efforts had failed. She'd failed. And now the kids would have a father who was more absent than ever. She wondered if they'd forgive her when they were older and realised what they'd missed out on.

Would they forgive Sam for putting the navy first or would they blame her for not compromising?

Would they realise their father could have compromised too or would they take his view and agree that he'd been asked to make sacrifices, not compromises?

'Is it okay if I take them out for dinner tonight? I'm only on leave until tomorrow.' Sam's question interrupted her musings.

'You've only got twenty-four hours?' Sam nodded. 'Why did you come?' Juliet asked. 'You didn't have to, you know. We don't have to be here in person.'

'I know. But I wasn't going to pass up my last opportunity to see my wife.'

'What do you mean?'

Sam turned slightly on his chair so he was facing her more directly. 'This is it, Jules. We're getting divorced. Next time I see you you'll be my ex-wife, and I know I've missed a lot of things in all the years we've been together but I'm not about to let our marriage end in my absence.'

She wanted to stamp her feet and yell and scream. If only Sam had been prepared to make

more of an effort to participate when they had
been married, perhaps it wouldn't have come to
this.

'So, can I take the kids or do you have plans?'

Juliet wanted to say, no, he couldn't take the
kids. She wanted to make it difficult. She wanted
to remind Sam that it was his choice to be a
part-time father but she knew that would achieve
nothing.

'We don't have plans. They'd love to go with
you.' And they would. There was no reason for
them not to spend time with their father. She
wasn't going to become one of those single mothers who denied children time with their father
out of spite. She wasn't spiteful and she was to
blame for this situation as much as Sam. They'd
both been too stubborn to back down. That's
what had brought them here.

'Taylor versus Taylor.' The bailiff called their
case.

Sam and Juliet stood and followed the
bailiff into the courtroom to stand before the
magistrate.

The courtroom was in marginally better condition than the waiting area but still small and

unimpressive. Juliet wasn't sure what she'd expected but something a bit grander, a bit more official in appearance would have suited the occasion better in her opinion. If it weren't for the raised bench where the magistrate was sitting, one could be forgiven for thinking they were in a school classroom circa 1980. At least the magistrate in her robes lent some formality to the occasion but the room itself was far from grand and in Juliet's opinion it was diminishing the event. Not that she wanted the event celebrated but she wanted to be able to look back on their twelve-year marriage with positive thoughts and this sombre, dull, drab room was taking the gloss off those years.

The magistrate nodded at them before saying, 'State your names, please.'

Juliet opened her mouth to speak but no words came out. She heard Sam's rich voice beside her—'Samuel Edward Taylor'—and that gave her the courage to state her own name, although her voice quivered with nerves. 'Juliet Ann Taylor.'

'You're filing for divorce?'

'Yes, Your Honour.' To Juliet's relief, Sam answered. She'd done about as much talking as she was capable of. Her knees were weak and she wasn't sure how long she'd be able to hold herself up. Her palms were sweaty and her mouth was dry.

'It says in your petition there are two minors. Have satisfactory custody arrangements been made for the children?' the magistrate asked.

'Yes, Your Honour.' Sam repeated his words.

'All right. Your application is granted. Your divorce becomes absolute one month and one day from now and the paperwork will be posted to you. Next case.'

That's it? Juliet was dumbfounded. Twelve years of marriage, dissolved in fewer than one hundred words. Sam turned and started walking away from the magistrate. Juliet followed him, feeling completely disoriented.

Sam walked the length of the courtroom and kept walking until he'd passed through the waiting chamber and into the corridor. Only then did he stop and turn to her.

'Is it always that quick?' he asked.

'I don't know,' she said. 'It's the first time I've got divorced.'

Sam smiled and her stomach trembled in

response. 'I thought she'd ask a few more questions.'

Juliet shrugged. Now that she thought about it there wasn't any reason for discussion with the magistrate. 'She's not a counsellor. As far as she's concerned, as long as we've filled in the application properly and made arrangements for the kids, she doesn't care. We're not contesting anything. She was probably glad to have a straightforward case.' She was irritated with herself over her reaction to Sam's smile and her annoyance had made her respond abruptly. But it wasn't Sam's fault she still found him attractive and she attempted to tone down her snappiness. 'But I know what you mean. It doesn't feel real, does it?'

'I guess it won't until we get the paperwork,' he replied.

Juliet didn't believe that would make any difference. So much of their day-to-day life would remain unchanged, continuing as it had for the past year, if not longer. She'd missed Sam when they'd been married and she expected to still miss him. She didn't expect much to change. The children would probably see just as much of him as they always had but she'd wanted him around more. That was what had started this whole process but now all that would change was that he wouldn't be coming home to her.

She knew that, at least initially, she'd be the only one who'd feel like something was missing. Sam had his career, his whole other life, and the children were still young enough to be oblivious to all the grown-up worries surrounding them. It was fair to say that Juliet didn't feel as though this situation had turned out quite as she'd planned.

Sam started walking, heading for the main foyer and the exit. 'Do you need a lift? I'm going to grab a taxi to the hotel.'

'No, thank you. Maggie will pick me up, I just need to call her.'

He stopped and turned to her. 'I'm sorry, Jules. Sorry it's come to this.' He leant down and placed his hand on her forearm as he kissed her on the cheek. His hand and lips were warm and her skin burned where he touched her. 'I'll see you around five-thirty when I pick up the kids.'

Juliet nodded, the lump in her throat preventing her from talking.

Sam left her then. Left her standing in the foyer, alone. Juliet watched him go and only once he was out of sight did she let her composure slip. She collapsed onto a nearby bench and let all the day's emotions pour out of her in a torrent of silent tears. She'd felt close to tears all day but she'd refused to let anyone see her cry. Not the children, not her sister, and especially not Sam. She searched her handbag for the packet of tissues she knew was in there as she wondered what had happened to their dreams, their plans for the future. But she knew what had happened. Sam had changed the rules and she had gambled and lost. She'd have to learn to live with that.

CHAPTER TWO

'DAD's here, Dad's here.'

Juliet could hear Edward yelling. He'd been sitting at the front window since five o'clock, waiting for Sam to arrive—he'd never sat still for that long in his life. Now Sam was here and Edward was running around the house like a maniac. Thirty minutes of inactivity was obviously far too long for a five-year-old boy!

Juliet answered Sam's knock at the door. He'd changed out of his uniform and was now wearing jeans and a pale green polo shirt. Juliet didn't recognise the shirt and she wondered when he'd bought it. Sam never shopped, he spent so much time in a uniform he said he didn't need many civvies so Juliet had always bought his clothes for him. Who was choosing them for him now? The shade of green was a perfect foil for Sam's tanned skin and highlighted his green eyes. Juliet couldn't imagine Sam choosing the shirt deliberately so he either got lucky with the colour or someone else bought it for him. It wasn't her business any more but she couldn't stop the flash of jealousy that raced through her.

She stepped back to invite Sam in just as Edward hurtled past her, launching himself at Sam like a little blond rocket. Sam caught him easily, scooping him up against his broad chest and carrying him inside. Juliet had been wondering whether or not to greet Sam with a kiss on the cheek but Edward's body formed a wall between them, taking that option out of the equation. Had they just set a precedent for all future greetings?

'Where's your sister?' Sam asked Edward.

'Dunno.'

'She's in her room,' Juliet replied, and Sam veered right, carrying Ed into Kate's room.

'Here's my gorgeous girl—are you ready for dinner?'

Juliet followed behind them, stopping in the doorway. Kate was still getting ready—aged eight, she already spent more time in front of the mirror than Juliet did. She was sliding a clip into her brown hair and Juliet smiled, Kate had been doing her hair for the last ten minutes, trying out different styles with varying accessories—clips, headbands and bows—but Sam's arrival seemed to have sped up the process. Kate finished her hair and grabbed her swing coat before crossing the room to greet her father with a hug and a kiss.

'Where are we going?' Edward asked.

'Sofia's.'

Juliet's throat was tight and hot tears stung her eyes. Eating at Sofia's Italian restaurant was a family tradition and it hurt to find that the tradition was going to continue without her. She blinked back tears, desperate to stop them from spilling over onto her cheeks. She couldn't believe she was still so wound up, she would have thought she'd cried enough earlier in the day to last her a while.

'Yay! Can I have *gelati*?'

Sam laughed and punched Edward lightly on the arm, immediately starting a play fight. 'Spaghetti first and then *gelati*.'

Juliet let Edward wrestle his father for a minute before calling a stop to the physical stuff. 'Okay, enough, guys,' she said. 'Time for dinner.'

'Your mum's right, champ,' Sam said as Edward started to complain that their game had been halted prematurely. 'The taxi's waiting.'

Juliet hadn't considered how Sam had got to their house but as she herded them through the front door and into the driveway she saw a cab parked behind her car. 'You can take my car if that's easier. I don't need it.'

'Aren't you coming with us?' Kate picked up on Juliet's wording.

'No, darling, this is Dad's treat.'

Sam stopped, extending her an invitation. 'You're welcome to join us, Jules.'

'Thanks, but there's some stuff I want to do here. Let me get the car keys.' She turned away from Sam, not wanting him to see the lie on her face. She grabbed her keys from the hall table and returned to find Sam had sent the taxi off. She handed him the keys and kissed her children goodbye. She watched them climb into her car and waited as they waved to her before they disappeared down the street.

She turned, picking up a stray football that was lying in the front garden, and took it inside with her, the vision of Edward's fair head stuck in her mind. He was the spitting image of Sam to look at, a little ball of muscle. They were both bundles of energy and Ed was already mad about ball sports, although, living in Melbourne, he preferred Aussie rules football over Sam's choice of rugby union.

Juliet had grown up in Sydney where rugby was the main winter sport, and although she hadn't been a huge fan she now had a soft spot for rugby as that was how she'd first met Sam. She moved through the house, tidying up bits and pieces as she let her mind wander.

She was still finding it difficult to reconcile herself with the idea that Sam was no longer her husband. He would always be part of her life, connected to her through their children, and she needed to work out how they were going to deal with that. After twelve years of marriage she couldn't expect to accept that it was over without some regrets but she knew she had to get past that.

The house was quiet, too quiet, but she had to be prepared to be alone. She wasn't exactly looking forward to having the house to herself but she thought the solitude might at least give her a chance to make some sense of the day.

In some respects twelve years seemed to have passed in the blink of an eye. Mostly, if it weren't for the changes she saw in her children and for the strands of grey appearing in her dark hair, changes that made it hard to ignore the passage of time, she wouldn't believe she was nearer forty than thirty.

Other days she felt all of her thirty-six years. Today was one of those days. She felt tired, physically and mentally. She wasn't surprised to be emotionally exhausted. It wasn't every day one had to appear in court to get divorced but if she was honest with herself she'd have to admit that she was often physically tired by early evening. Realistically she knew it had nothing to do with being a single mother, she'd been a single mother for long stretches of time when Sam had been away on naval exercises, but she hadn't been able to pinpoint any other change, except perhaps stress. She should probably go and get a check-up, she thought, she couldn't afford to get sick.

She took some clean laundry into her room. Her bed was freshly made, the pillows plumped and inviting. The house was still. It couldn't hurt to lie down for a few minutes, could it? Maybe a catnap would lift her spirits.

She lay down, trying to remember what she'd looked like thirteen years ago when she'd first met Sam. It was easier to recall exactly what he'd looked like. A gorgeous, blond Adonis, and it had been lust at first sight. She'd been twenty-four and had moved from Sydney to Canberra, the nation's capital, to do her Master's in international law at the Australian National University. Her flatmate, Stella, had dragged her to a rugby game between the engineering faculty of the ANU and a team from the defence force academy. It had been an annual event, a huge social day with the rugby match followed by a party, and Stella had been chasing one of the university players, so Juliet had been her moral support. Juliet had expected to help Stella meet her man, she hadn't expected to find one for herself.

Canberra, 1995

Juliet was standing with Stella and a group of friends on the boundary of the rugby pitch when a man, a glorious, blond man, raced towards them, flying down the wing. He had the ball tucked under his right arm and his rugby jumper was moulded to his body. Juliet could see the outline of his biceps and deltoid clearly defined by the contours of his top. She was a sucker for good arms and there was no doubt that this guy had them. She watched as he fended off an opposing player with his left hand, a quick shove to the chest upsetting his opponent's balance, and he was away, strong legs pumping as he headed for the try-line. He goose-stepped over a diving defender, his quick movements belying his size. He had to be at least six feet of solid muscle but he moved with the agility of someone much lighter.

Juliet could see the last line of defence, a pair of opponents, blocking his path, lining up to double-team him. She saw him look around quickly, assessing his options. He had a teammate coming up on his outside. He didn't slow his pace but ran in a slightly diagonal line towards the centre of the pitch, straight towards the oncoming defenders. Juliet held her breath, willing this glorious stranger safely past them. She couldn't see how he could possibly manage to evade them—as solid as he was, the others were bigger again and there were two of them. They had the typical build of rugby players—massive limbs, thick necks and take-no-prisoners looks on their faces. They looked like two enormous tree trunks in the middle of the field.

Juliet waited, expecting to see the blond demi-god attempt to dodge around the opposition—she was convinced he'd be fast enough to get around them but he kept running straight at them. She watched him drop his left shoulder and spin to his right as the full backs crunched into him, slamming him into the ground. Even on the soft grass the thud of bodies colliding was loud and painful. Her hands flew to her mouth—somewhere under that man mountain lay the most divine male she'd seen in a long time—how many pieces was he going to be in when the dust settled?

She felt someone bump against her, the crowd around her was screaming and yelling, people were jumping up and down. She saw the ball come sailing backwards, arcing through the air. Had he managed to release the ball before he'd been crunched?

The diagonal path he'd chosen, the path that had led him straight into danger, had given his teammate a chance to gain some ground and Juliet watched as the ball landed securely in the teammate's hands. He was ten metres from the opposing try line with no one to beat.

Juliet celebrated the try with the crowd, caught up in the moment, caught up in one man. She nudged Stella as the celebrations continued. 'Do you know who number fourteen is for the defence force?'

Stella shook her head. Juliet wasn't surprised; Stella was there to cheer for the university side— she had no allegiance to the defence academy. But that didn't mean Juliet couldn't adopt the defence force team as hers.

'Can I have a look at the programme?' she asked.

Stella handed over the paper she'd been holding and Juliet scrolled down the page. Number fourteen—Sam Taylor. It wasn't much, but it was better than nothing.

Juliet spent the rest of the half with one eye on Sam and the other on the crowd, trying to determine if anyone seemed to be following Sam particularly. There were plenty of supporters yelling for him whenever he got the ball, which seemed to be a frequent occurrence, but it was hard to tell if any of them were as focussed on Sam as she was. In the end she gave up and spent the rest of the time enjoying the spectacle and vowing to introduce herself to him after the match.

The spectators gathered in the university rugby club bar at the end of the game and wasted no time before ordering drinks. Juliet was careful to stay in control. The rugby players had all gone to shower and change and she wanted to be prepared for Sam's return. She was going to make sure she made a good first impression, for reasons she didn't fully understand but which seemed vitally important.

She and Stella positioned themselves between the band and the bar and kept an eye on the doors. The players were beginning to drift in now. They were easy to pick out of the crowd as most still had damp hair from their showers. The university boys were in civvies but the defence force boys were in their dress uniforms.

In Juliet's opinion the defence force boys had an unfair advantage over the university boys. Dress uniforms trumped casual clothes any day.

Sam came through the doors, his white uniform immaculate. She'd always been a sucker for a man in uniform. He was six feet of muscle impeccably dressed. His hair was damp from the shower so it was a darker blond now, thick and wavy. Juliet wondered if there was a regulation about hair length in the navy. Sam's hair looked longer than most, although it stopped short of his collar. His shoulders were broad and straight and he looked like a perfect gentleman, strong and protective, chivalrous. Juliet knew he might be none of those things but he could certainly sell the illusion.

She scanned the room, waiting to see if anyone went to claim him. A couple of his companions broke away to meet their girlfriends but Sam continued walking. From her spot on the far side of the room she could see him sweep his gaze across the crowd. Was he looking for anyone in particular? He hadn't stopped scanning the room and she was concentrating so intently on his movements that she was unprepared when his gaze swept her side of the room. Before she had a chance to look away their eyes locked. She tried to relax. After all, he couldn't know she'd been watching him ever since he'd stepped inside, and she thought she'd pulled it off until he winked at her. She felt herself blush and was tempted to dive behind Stella, but at least he'd noticed her. That was a good thing, so she smiled at him before looking away. She still had time to play it cool and work out her plan of attack.

She waited until he was at the bar then offered to fetch Stella another drink.

'Excuse me, would you mind if I squeezed in here?' People were packed tightly together along the bar, giving her the perfect excuse to cram herself in beside Sam.

'Not at all,' he said, moving over to make space for her. He smiled at her and Juliet felt her heart skip a beat. She'd always thought that was just a saying but there was no other way to describe the effect of his smile on her. If he was gorgeous when he was running around a rugby field, he was absolutely superb when he smiled. His smile was wide and white and started at the right-hand corner of his mouth before spreading to the left and finally reaching his eyes. Crinkles appeared in the corners of his eyes, but they didn't detract from his looks. He looked like a man who smiled often and easily. The moment his smile lit up his face Juliet knew she was in big trouble. Sam had to be hers—there were no two ways about it.

Her eyes were still locked on his as she thanked him for making room. 'I enjoyed the game. Congratulations on winning.' She paused for a fraction before deciding nothing ventured, nothing gained. 'It's Sam, isn't it? I'm Juliet,' she said, holding out her hand.

He shook her hand and Juliet had the strangest sense of déjà vu. His touch was familiar but she knew that was impossible, yet she could sense a memory, almost as though her skin had felt his touch before. It was slightly unnerving but Juliet couldn't force herself to remove her hand.

'Have we met before?' Sam asked. He was frowning and a crease appeared between his eyes.

'No.' Had he felt the same strange familiarity or was he only asking because she'd used his name? She could explain one reason but not the other. 'I looked you up in the match programme after that first try. I wanted to know who every-one was cheering for.' Juliet let go of his hand.

He smiled again, his right-to-left smile, and said, 'What about you? Who were you cheering for?'

'No one really…not for the first fifteen minutes anyway. I came with a girlfriend to cheer for the uni team but I might have swapped allegiances.' She gave him a sideways glance, hoping he'd pick up on her invitation.

'So you don't have a boyfriend on the uni team who's going to get upset if I buy you a drink?'

'No boyfriend.'

And that had been it. Somewhere along the way Juliet had remembered to give Stella her drink and had been relieved to find her in a group that included the boy she was keen on, but after that Sam had been the only one who had held any interest for Juliet.

They'd had such passion and she still found it hard to believe that it hadn't been enough to sustain them. Hard to believe they hadn't made it.

She'd only ever had eyes for Sam but passion was no match for reality.

* * *

The sound of the front door opening brought Juliet out of her reverie. Initially she thought Sam and the children were home but then she heard Maggie calling her. Her sister had gone for a run and was now probably wondering where everyone had disappeared to. The house was in darkness as Juliet hadn't turned any lights on and it probably seemed abandoned.

'In here, Mags,' she called out, letting Maggie know she was home.

Maggie stuck her head into Juliet's room. 'What are you doing?'

'Nothing,' Juliet said as she sat up.

'It's very quiet. Are the kids already in bed?'

'No, Sam's taken them out for dinner.'

'He's still in town?'

'He goes back tomorrow,' Juliet said.

'And then what?' Maggie crossed the room and sat on the bed beside Juliet.

'I'm not sure. That's what I've been thinking about. Where do I go from here? On one hand nothing's changed but on the other...'

'Everything's changed.'

Juliet nodded.

'You could have gone with him.'

'I could have but moving every three years or, worse, every six months wasn't the right thing for the children, especially Kate. Regardless of her issues, moving constantly once we had a family wasn't our plan and I thought that given the childhood Sam had he'd want to keep his family together. I thought it would be important to him. But the navy was more important and Sam couldn't, or wouldn't, give it up.' Juliet picked at the quilt cover as she spoke. 'I made him choose between the navy and us, and I lost.' She shrugged. 'No point sitting here feeling sorry for myself. I'll just have to get on with things.'

Maggie hugged her. 'You know I'll always be here if you need me.'

'Thanks, but I can't expect you to jump on a plane and fly down to Melbourne at the drop of a hat. You're here now and I do appreciate that but I'm an adult, and I should be able to manage on my own.'

'You can manage but there will be times when it's tough to do that and Sam won't always be able to help you with the kids in a crisis—he could be on the other side of the world. I'll only be in Sydney so if you need me, I want to know. You've done it for me and I'd be upset to think you wouldn't call me. Okay?'

Juliet nodded. 'Thanks, Mags.'

Maggie squeezed her shoulders. 'No probs. Now, can I make you a cup of tea before I jump in the shower?'

'No, I'm fine really. The kids should be back soon. Have a shower while there's still some peace and quiet.'

Maggie disappeared into the guest bathroom and was still in there when Sam and the children returned. Juliet met them at the door and Sam handed her the car keys and a pizza box. 'We thought you probably hadn't eaten. It's a Margherita.'

'Thank you,' she said as she took the box from Sam's hands. Margherita was her favourite. Sam had always been good at the little things but it was the big things that had torn them apart. He could remember her favourite pizza topping and how she liked her tea but couldn't understand why she didn't want to move house every three years for the rest of her life.

Let it go, she reprimanded herself, *it's over.*

She took the pizza into the kitchen and she could hear the children asking Sam to tuck them into bed before he left. She let Sam help them brush their teeth, change into their pyjamas and read them a story while she ate a couple of slices of pizza, leaving some for Maggie. When the children were ready for bed she stood and watched as Sam kissed them goodnight, amazed as always that she and Sam had created two incredible little people. Two miniature versions of themselves.

But the similarities between her and her daughter were physical rather than psychological. Kate, with her thick dark hair and bright blue eyes, was the spitting image of herself at the same age but she was far more reserved than Juliet had ever been. Juliet was stubborn and headstrong and prone to making quick decisions; Kate was far more measured and in control of her emotions, even at the age of eight. Juliet sometimes wondered if Kate's dyslexia had influenced her personality. Had she learned to take her time with her responses to ensure she made fewer mistakes or was she simply less volatile than her mother?

Edward and Kate were as different as chalk and cheese, both in looks and behaviour. Edward had inherited his father's looks and much of his personality. They were both adrenalin junkies, both attracted to danger. She was constantly on the lookout around Edward because he was still too young to assess risk. Sam liked order and routine, he liked to follow the rules and would never make a rash judgement. Juliet hoped Ed would develop some of his father's sense as he matured but she was worried because she suspected Sam might have always had that slightly sensible gene and that healthy regard for the rules may have been reinforced by his defence force upbringing. Sam's love of order and routine had certainly helped him to cope with the frequent moves that he'd been exposed to as a defence force brat. From what he ate for breakfast and how he read the paper to the system in his wardrobe and in his bookshelves, Sam was a creature of habit. Even the kids' bedtime routine had been started by Sam. And now Juliet had taken away some of that.

She followed Sam's lead, kissing the children goodnight as an unwelcome thought burrowed its way into her head—other than their children, they hadn't made much of a success of their life together.

CHAPTER THREE

August 2008

JULIET was rushing around the house, trying to get several last-minute jobs out of the way before fetching Edward from kindergarten, when she was interrupted by a knock at the door. A postman waited with a letter, registered mail. She showed the postman her driver's licence as identification and signed for the envelope with a shaky hand. She knew what the envelope contained—it could only be one thing. It had been a month and a day since she and Sam had been in court.

This was it. Her self-imposed D-Day.

She'd been delaying a whole host of things, things she couldn't put off any longer. She hadn't set a date exactly but she'd decided that once the divorce was final and she had the paperwork that said so, she would have to face facts.

She took the envelope to the kitchen and slit it open with a knife.

It had been a month and a day since she'd seen Sam, one month and a day since they'd been in court. Her divorce was absolute. It was there in black and white in front of her. She was now officially a divorcee.

Before she could procrastinate again or let herself be distracted by the children, she did the two things she'd been avoiding. She slid her wedding and engagement rings off her finger and slipped them onto her right hand. It was a slightly tighter fit but she wasn't ready to be without them totally, though she also had no cause to still be wearing them on her left hand. The rings felt heavy on her right hand and her thumb automatically fiddled with the bands. She supposed she'd get used to the sensation.

One more task to do. She picked up the phone but hesitated before dialling. She put it onto the kitchen bench while she deliberated. What if she didn't need to make this phone call after all? She palpated her left breast with her fingers, hoping, once again, that maybe the lump had disappeared. But it was still there, about the size of a small walnut. She retrieved the phone and made a long-overdue appointment with her doctor.

'Good morning, Juliet,' Dr Wilson said as she called her into the consulting room. 'What can I do for you today?'

'I've found another breast lump,' Juliet said as she sat down. She had a history of benign nodules and she'd had various tests done in the past but thankfully they'd all come back negative for any malignancy.

'When did you notice this one?'

'A few months ago,' she answered honestly.

'Any changes in this one?'

'I think it's got bigger.'

Dr Wilson looked at her with one eyebrow raised. 'Any reason why you haven't been in to see me sooner?'

Juliet knew that the change in the size of the lump should have sounded warning bells. It had, she just hadn't had the time or energy to deal with it. Part of her had also tried to pretend that this lump was just like all the others and they'd been fine, hadn't they? But she knew that this lump wasn't the same—it had kept on growing.

'Sam and I got divorced. I had a lot on my plate.'

'I'm sorry to hear about the divorce—that must have been tough.' Dr Wilson paused before adding, 'Do you want my lecture on how important it is not to neglect your health now or should I save it for later?'

Juliet shook her head. 'Save it. I know I owe it to my children to look after myself, that's why I'm here.'

'Fair enough. Let's have a look at this lump, then, shall we?'

Juliet undressed and was poked and prodded for the first of what would become many times over the course of the next few days. The lump was tender but no worse than the others had been.

'How big was it when you first noticed it?' Dr Wilson asked.

'About the size of a pea,' Juliet recalled.

'Just under a centimetre, then. It's now between three and four. When did you notice that it had got bigger?'

'Probably five or six weeks ago,' Juliet estimated. It had been around the time she and Sam had gone to court, which was one reason she'd ignored it. It hadn't reached the top of her list of priorities yet.

'I think we need to check this out further. You can get dressed and then I'll take some blood, and I'm also going to send you off for a mammogram. You haven't had one before, have you?'

'No, only ultrasounds.'

'It can be a bit difficult to get a clear picture with a mammogram in the under forty-five age group because your breast tissue is still quite dense, but I want to do that so we can get a look at the size and shape of the lump and a clear idea of its position. I'm going to refer you for a biopsy as well but those results will take a little longer to get back.'

Juliet was dressed now and sat in the chair beside Dr. Wilson's desk, extending her left arm, ready for blood to be drawn. The needle stung as it entered her arm and she watched the dark red blood fill up the vial, wondering what sort of nasty things her blood was harbouring.

'I want you to have the mammogram this

afternoon, and I'll make some calls and see if I can get you in for the biopsy tomorrow,' Dr Wilson said as she capped and labelled Juliet's blood. 'Is there someone who can help you with the children if the appointment times clash with school pick-ups? It might make it easier to get appointments for you if you can be flexible.'

Juliet nodded silently. She didn't have a clue who to call but she was sure she'd think of someone once her brain had time to process all the other stuff Dr Wilson was talking about. Mammograms, biopsies, blood tests. She hadn't actually said the word yet but Juliet knew what she was thinking. Cancer.

Juliet was struggling to get past that word. The word was stuck in her head, making it very difficult to concentrate on everything else Dr Wilson was telling her. The word was also stuck in her throat, making it difficult to breathe. Perhaps she'd feel better if that word was out in the open.

'You think I have cancer?'

Saying it out loud didn't improve matters much. She was breathing now but the tightness in her chest had been replaced by nausea.

Dr Wilson's reply didn't ease her fears. 'I think this lump is different from the fibroadenomas you already have. It's presenting more like a tumour because it's growing rapidly and I don't like that. I think we need to get as much information as we can to determine what we're dealing with but, remember, not all lumps are malignant.'

Juliet nodded but nothing else changed—she still felt nauseous, she still had a new lump in her breast.

'Do you want to call someone now? Get someone to drive you to the breast-screening clinic?' Dr Wilson asked.

'No, I'm okay, I'll drive myself,' Juliet replied, thinking that she needed to get through the mammogram as quickly as possible to make sure she was in time to collect the children from kindy and school.

'Okay. But can you arrange for someone to drive you to the biopsy? Your chest is likely to be quite sore once the local anaesthetic wears off and you'd be wise not to drive.'

Juliet nodded and left Dr Wilson's surgery with referrals for the mammogram and the biopsy and a follow-up appointment for two days hence. The receptionist would ring her with a time for the biopsy.

The mammogram was not the horrific experience she had been anticipating, judging from comments she'd heard from other women over the years. It was uncomfortable but in the scheme of things it was bearable.

Maybe she was in shock, numb to what was happening around her. She felt as though she was in a nightmare. The whole day had a surreal quality to it and she half expected one of the children to wake her up at any minute. Trying to take on board everything that she was being told was proving difficult when she felt as though she was wading through thick fog. Nothing was making sense. Was it really possible that she had cancer?

She tried to think through the situation but it was virtually impossible, partly because she had no facts yet and partly because she couldn't believe it was really happening.

She got dressed after the mammogram and hoped she was giving all the right responses as the technicians gave her more information, but her mind had already moved on to the next day and to the arrangements she would have to make. There was a message on her phone with the appointment time for the biopsy. Who would drive her to her next appointment? Perhaps she should take a taxi. Who could she ask to collect the children? She knew that this might only be the beginning of a host of favours she could need from people. If there was bad news then Dr Wilson was right—she was going to need support. Where was this going to come from?

She put those thoughts to the back of her mind while she drove to the kindergarten to collect Edward, focussing on the road and on getting there safely.

Edward's face lit up with a delightful smile, Sam's smile, when he saw her waiting to collect him—it was as though her presence was a big surprise. She wondered who would collect him if something happened to her and then quickly pushed that thought to the back of her mind as she hugged Ed to her when he arrived at her feet at full speed. He was closely followed by his best friends, Jake and Rory—they'd met on their first day of three-year-old kindergarten and were almost always together, like the three musketeers. Their mothers, Anna and Gabby, had become good friends of Juliet's by association and she wondered if their friendship would stretch a little further if she needed their help.

She saw Gabby arriving to collect Rory, running late as usual. Gabby waved and came straight over to Juliet. 'Hi, how are you? Rory was wondering if Ed would like to come for a play. Would that suit you?' Gabby asked, not pausing for breath. She always did things at a fast pace and was always busy, and Juliet sometimes wondered if she ever slept.

'Is there any chance you could have him tomorrow instead?' Juliet hated asking but if Gabby was offering to have Edward surely she wouldn't mind if it was tomorrow and not today? 'I need to have some tests done and I'm not supposed to drive afterwards.'

The boys, sensing that their mothers weren't in a hurry to leave, had made a beeline for the playground adjacent the kindergarten. Gabby and Juliet wandered in that direction too.

'Are you having eye tests?' Gabby asked.

Juliet knew that eye tests often involved eyedrops that dilated pupils, making driving difficult.

She wished it was something that simple. She supposed she should explain; she would end up telling Gabby at some point anyway as she was sure to need her help. 'No. I have to have a biopsy. I found a lump in my breast.'

Juliet heard Gabby's sharp intake of breath and saw her eyes widen. 'When did this happen?'

'I noticed it a while back but I was at the doctor today.'

'And you're straight in for a biopsy?'

Juliet knew Gabby was considering the timeline, recognising the sense of urgency. 'I had a mammogram today. My GP wants the information as quickly as possible.'

'Have you got any info yet?'

Juliet shook her head. 'No, the mammogram results will go straight to my GP and to the surgeon for tomorrow.'

'How are you getting to tomorrow's appointment?' Gabby was firing questions at Juliet, once again barely pausing for breath.

'I'll catch a cab.'

'Why don't I drive you? I'll make sure you get home and then I'll pick up the boys and Kate and bring them home later.'

'What about work?'

Gabby waved a hand, dismissing Juliet's protests. 'Finn's around. I'll just tell him he'll need to manage the gallery—it doesn't need both of us there.'

Gabby and her husband owned an upmarket art gallery and travelled frequently. Juliet started to protest and then stopped herself. As much as she didn't like to ask for help, she would have to get used to it, just as she would have to get used to accepting help when it was offered. 'If you're sure, that would be fabulous. I'm a bit apprehensive.'

'Of course you are, anyone would be, but I'm sure it will all be fine.'

Juliet wished she could be so certain. She was expecting bad news, she could almost feel it coming, but she didn't comment. She called to Edward, told him they needed to collect Kate, and then gave Gabby the details of where and when the appointment was, and agreed to be ready an hour before.

The next week was a whirlwind of appointments. Juliet saw the specialist and had a core biopsy under a local anaesthetic; she had a follow-up with her GP and then went back to the specialist. It was all she could do to keep track of which doctor she was seeing on which day, which hospital she had to be at and which forms she needed to take with her, without having to worry about the routine things like feeding the children. Fortunately Gabby was fabulous. She stepped in and basically ran Juliet's life for her, taking over all the general household chores and giving Juliet time to deal with the doctors and to hug her children. Over the next week Gabby alternated between being Juliet's taxi service, nanny, personal shopper and cook, but even Gabby couldn't stop the downward spiral that was Juliet's medical condition.

Seven days after the mammogram the specialist delivered the diagnosis and it was just as Juliet had feared. The lump she'd been ignoring for several months was a malignant tumour.

She had breast cancer.

Juliet's world was crumbling around her. She had two small children and she was on her own. She was divorced. She had breast cancer.

She wanted her old life back. She wanted her health back. She wanted Sam.

Gabby was supportive. Once again she cooked dinner for Juliet's children on the night Juliet got her diagnosis and she offered to cook for Juliet too, but she couldn't eat. She couldn't imagine that she'd ever feel like eating again.

Gabby did what she could but she wasn't Sam.

She'd offered to stay, had offered to keep Juliet company after the children had been put to bed, but Juliet had said she wanted to be alone.

She'd lied.

What Juliet wanted was Sam.

Sam was her rock. He had got her through her first crisis, her first two crises. She remembered how Sam had been there for her nine years ago and she knew she wouldn't have managed without him. Who would be her rock now?

Darwin, 1999

Juliet carried the last of the shopping bags into the house. It was a humid, steamy day, typical Darwin dry-season weather, and she could feel the beads of sweat trickling down between her breasts. She unpacked the groceries, putting the things that had to go into the fridge away before deciding to leave the rest until after her swim.

She and Sam had moved directly from wintry Canberra to the tropics of the Northern Territory. It had taken her a while to acclimatise to the tropical Darwin weather but she'd finally learned to slow her pace to suit the climate. Things moved more slowly in the north. It was something the rest of the country always commented on and Juliet could understand why—it was impossible to maintain a hectic schedule in these hot, moist, stupefying temperatures.

They'd lived in Darwin for nearly three years now and because of the city's transient population they were almost considered locals. Being part of the defence force had made the transition relatively easy. Defence force personnel were accustomed to people coming and going and were generally a sociable, welcoming group of people. They had settled easily into the city. Juliet had completed her Master's in international law in Canberra and had gone on to complete a diploma in education as well. She was teaching at the law school at the university and through this network and the defence force they had a wide circle of acquaintances.

There was always something happening—a barbeque, a game of tennis, drinks for someone who was leaving or to welcome new arrivals—and Sam and Juliet had an active social life, but what Juliet really loved was when it was just her and Sam, together, their own little unit. They'd moved here as virtual newlyweds and Juliet still cherished the rare occasions when she had Sam to herself. It was an idyllic lifestyle and they existed in a state of euphoria and contentment. Only a few weeks ago, their little bubble had expanded when Juliet had got a positive result on a pregnancy test. She now had everything she'd ever wished for.

She finished putting away the groceries and went to find her bathers. It was an afternoon ritual for her to meet Sam at the swimming pool on the naval base for a late-afternoon swim and a game of tennis or a drink with whoever was around in the officers' mess. The base was only a five-minute drive from their married quarters and the trip was worth every second in this hot and humid climate.

Juliet found her swimsuit and changed out of her sundress. As she stepped out of her underwear she noticed some spots of blood. Just small spots, but surely that wasn't normal. Beside her bed was the bible of expectant mothers and, slightly panicked, Juliet grabbed the book, searching for information. What did the book say about spotting? Was there anything in there to reassure her?

Chapter two said some women got spotting in the first month of pregnancy around about the time their period would normally be due. The advice was to rest and see if the bleeding stopped. But Juliet was eleven weeks pregnant. She flipped through the book, frantically searching for more. Chapter seven talked about bleeding in the last few weeks of pregnancy but there was nothing in between. She found nothing that set her mind at ease. Swimming was obviously out of the question if there was bleeding. Rest seemed to be the answer. She lay on her bed and continued scouring her book for any more information as she willed herself to stay calm and relaxed and prayed for the bleeding to stop.

It didn't.

Calm and relaxed turned into stomach cramps. Juliet was almost too afraid to check but she had to know. She went to the bathroom. The bleeding was heavier and the blood was bright red. That wasn't good.

She phoned Sam and he was by her side within ten minutes. Fifteen minutes after that he'd whisked her off to the emergency department at the Darwin Hospital and she was being taken into a cubicle for an ultrasound scan. Sam held her hand as the technician started the consult and stayed beside her when the technician went to call for the doctor. Juliet felt her pulse increase its pace with nervousness. She wanted the technician to show her an image of the baby on the screen, not fetch the doctor. She'd read enough of her pregnancy book to know she should be able to see her baby on the monitor. The only thing that kept her from panicking, that prevented her from screaming and yelling and demanding to know what was wrong, was Sam's calming presence. She knew if he let go of her hand she would lose control. Somehow Sam knew that too and he held his position, comforting her with his solid, dependable presence. Maybe, just maybe, she thought, things would be okay as long as Sam was there.

The female doctor was young, too young to be completely reassuring, but she had a calm and confident manner that helped to put Juliet at ease.

'How far along are you?' the doctor asked as she moved the ultrasound over Juliet's abdomen.

'Eleven weeks.'

The doctor nodded and then pointed towards the ultrasound monitor. There was a little arrow that moved about the screen as she manipulated the mouse. 'Can you see that circle?' she asked. 'That's the foetal sac.'

Yes, Juliet thought, that's better. The doctor will be able to show me my baby. Maybe the technician was just having trouble finding it. But the doctor hadn't finished.

'I should be able to see a heartbeat within the sac but there's nothing there. Your baby hasn't developed.' The doctor removed the ultrasound transducer from Juliet's abdomen and wiped the gel off her stomach. 'I'm sorry.'

Juliet had no words of reply.

Sam wasn't quite as stunned. 'You're sorry?

What do you mean, you're sorry? We had a positive pregnancy test,' he said. A frown creased his forehead and Juliet knew he was trying to understand what the doctor was telling them. It wasn't making much sense to her either.

'You were pregnant but the pregnancy hasn't progressed,' the doctor explained.

'You're telling us there's no baby?'

The doctor nodded.

'What happened?' Sam asked.

'We never really know,' the doctor replied. 'It's impossible to tell at this stage—the foetus just stops developing. One in three babies don't make it. It's not uncommon, it's just that people don't talk about it much. Give yourself some time to heal and grieve and then you can try again. Most of the time there's no rhyme or reason for losing a baby, just like there's no reason to think things will go wrong next time.'

Juliet didn't say a word. She couldn't think about the next time, all she could think about was this baby they'd just lost. The doctor had called it a foetus, but it hadn't been a foetus, not to her. It had been their baby.

Sam took her home and put her to bed and held

her while she cried, held her while she mourned their child. He didn't try to tell her everything would be okay. It was too soon for that and Juliet loved him for being able to feel her loss. He felt it too.

A baby had been the next step in their life together. Juliet doted on her sister's children. Maggie had married and had had her children at a young age, and while Juliet loved her niece and nephew she'd never had a burning desire to have her own family until she'd met Sam. Everything had changed for her then. She'd found the man she wanted to spend the rest of her life with and that included the man who she wanted to be the father of her children. She'd been ecstatic to discover she was pregnant and now that had been taken away from her with no warning.

Sam had been just as excited. He was an only child and his mother had died when he'd still been quite young. While he was close to his father Juliet knew he loved the idea of creating his own family and she knew he was upset too. But Sam made it his priority to look after her and for the next few weeks Sam was her rock.

He organised sick leave for Juliet and took time

off work himself and they flew to Ubud on the Indonesian island of Bali, where they spent a week in the mountains. The villa Sam rented came with a housekeeper and a cook and Juliet regained her appetite on a diet of fresh fruit, lean meats, fish and salads. They walked every morning and spent the afternoon lying by their private pool.

Juliet still cried herself to sleep but Sam was there for her and after a few days Juliet's spirit started to recover. After four days Sam's crooked smile returned and that lifted Juliet's spirit even further.

After five days they ventured down the mountain into the hustle and bustle of beachside Kuta. Juliet had been apprehensive about the crowds but no one knew her and no one knew she'd just lost a baby. She looked no different to any of the other tourists and no one gave her a second glance. No one except the hawkers, but they weren't targeting her specifically, they targeted all the foreigners.

She found the hawkers overwhelming at first after the more relaxed shopkeepers of Ubud but Sam protected her from their frenzied persistence and Juliet eventually embraced the noise and the colour and, to a lesser extent, the crowds. The smells were a little harder to embrace but even those she eventually got accustomed to. She could have hidden away from the overwhelming vibrancy, she could have insisted that Sam take her back up the mountains, but instead, with Sam beside her, she absorbed the energy and felt it restore some life into her soul. With Sam beside her she survived the streets of Kuta and that felt like a major achievement. Not only had she survived but she was starting to come back to life, and Juliet knew she would be okay, knew that, as long as she had Sam, things would be all right.

They were back at their villa in time for dinner. Sitting beside the pool, surrounded by the scent of frangipani and dining by candlelight, they began to talk about the future again, to discuss their hopes and dreams for the family they would surely have. Slowly Juliet started to trust that their dreams were not over, just delayed.

A couple of days further on and she was ready to return to Darwin. She felt rested and, if still not fully recovered, at least able to face her life.

She understood that there wasn't always a reason for things and she trusted that children would be part of their lives when the time was right. Sam had given her comfort; he'd known how to help her heal, and while she never forgot this pregnancy she was able to get past the loss.

What she didn't know as she boarded the plane in Denpasar was that the miscarriage would be the first test of her resolve that year, but not the last.

One week later she received a call from her father. That in itself was unusual—her mother normally phoned and her dad would speak briefly once she and her mother had finished gossiping. Juliet immediately anticipated bad news and assumed it involved her mother. Why else would her father call? He reassured her that her mother was fine and he was calling about her brother-in-law, Maggie's husband, Steve.

Steve was a policeman in Sydney and he'd been called in as part of reinforcements when riots had broken out at a Sydney beach. Juliet had seen images on the evening news the previous day—temperatures were soaring in an early summer heatwave and some longstanding cultural differences had spilled over from verbal sparring into physical violence. Juliet had called Maggie to check on Steve and had been told he'd sustained a head injury but had been discharged from hospital. She'd relaxed and she relaxed again now—she'd only spoken to Maggie a few hours ago, she could reassure her father that all was well.

But her father had more recent news, and was calling to tell her that Steve had been readmitted to hospital during the night. He'd had a large subdural haematoma and had died before the neurosurgeon had reached the hospital.

Her sister Maggie was a widow.

Juliet and Sam were on the next flight to Sydney.

Sam had been worried that Steve's death would stretch Juliet to breaking point but for Juliet, Steve's death put things into perspective. Her loss paled in comparison to Maggie's. Thanks to Sam, Juliet had been able to escape to the sanctuary of Bali where she had been able to hide from her life until her sorrow over the miscarriage was able to be tucked away in her heart.

It was no longer completely overwhelming and all-consuming.

Maggie had lost her husband and she was left with two young children to comfort, explain to and care for. There was nowhere for Maggie to hide and despite Sam's concerns Juliet was able to embrace the responsibility of being the one to support and comfort Maggie.

She stayed in Sydney when Sam went back to Darwin but when she returned to Sam she was her old self, determined to move forward. They had each other and they would be okay, she'd make sure of it.

Throughout all of this, Sam had supported her and she knew she would never have made it through to the other side without him. He'd been her rock then but who would be her rock now?

CHAPTER FOUR

September 2008

IT HAD been several days since she'd finished having all the tests and since the oncologist had given her the bad news. It had taken Juliet a few days to get it all straight in her own head and some time to work out the best way to inform her family of the situation. She needed to make sure she had all the facts and information clear in her own mind before she attempted to explain it to others. She needed to make sense of the diagnosis, treatment and prognosis, and she felt it was important that she have control over who was told when.

Everyone who needed to know, other than the children, was in New South Wales—her parents, her sister and Sam. The best plan was to arrange a weekend visit, organising it as just a weekend away with no other agenda. There would be time for explanations when she arrived.

She phoned everyone and made arrangements. They would stay with Maggie for two nights and Juliet would tell her first. She was a nurse and Juliet expected her to cope best with the news. Sam was free on the second night and Juliet arranged for him to take the children out and that would give her a chance to see him. The next morning Maggie would drive Juliet and the children down to Bowral, where they would all spend the weekend with Juliet and Maggie's parents. Juliet wanted Maggie there for emotional support.

Maggie's weekend was the first that Juliet ruined but Maggie was stoic and more than happy to give Juliet whatever support she needed in whatever form. Juliet had expected nothing less from her older sister but it was comforting to know that Maggie would be there for her. Now it was Sam's turn to hear the news.

Sam opened Maggie's gate and walked up the narrow path to the front door. Maggie had lived here for as long as he'd known her. He knew that originally Maggie and her husband Steve had planned to buy something bigger as their children got older, but that had been before Steve had died. Maggie hadn't wanted to move after that; she'd wanted to stay where her memories were. Sam was pleased—there were lots of happy memories for him here too. He and Juliet had spent plenty of holidays and Christmas times here with their children and their cousins and Sam didn't have any regrets about that. Just walking through the gate put a smile on his face, and knowing he was about to see his kids for the first time in several weeks made the walk even sweeter.

He knocked on the door and waited to hear the sound of children's footsteps running up the passage, echoing on the wooden floorboards. But the steps he heard were quieter and much more even. The door opened and Juliet was standing there. Just Juliet.

He frowned. Where were the kids? The house was small so he should have been able to hear their noise.

'Hello, Sam, come in.'

'Juliet.' He was distracted by the silence and just managed to remember to return her greeting.

He looked past her, searching for the children, but there was no sound and no movement.

Juliet stepped aside, making space for him to enter the house, and he looked properly at her for the first time as he moved through the doorway. She looked different. She was tiny, almost a foot shorter than him, and the top of her head barely reached his shoulder. She was barefoot, which made her seem even smaller, but her height wasn't the difference as she'd always been little.

Had she changed her hairstyle? He didn't think so—her thick chestnut hair still fell past her shoulders and framed her petite, heart-shaped face. She had delicate features and the most amazing blue eyes, and those were as striking as ever.

He followed her down the passage to the kitchen at the rear of the house. Had she lost weight? Was that the difference? She'd never been fat but she was normally curvy and she looked thinner than he remembered. From behind she was still the same hourglass shape, her bottom still round and firm, but she was definitely thinner.

He listened for the sound of the children as he

walked. Nothing but silence. He frowned. He had the right day and time, he was certain of that. 'Where are the kids?'

'Maggie's taken them to a movie. They'll be back in an hour or so.'

Sam was annoyed. He'd made a promise to himself that he'd be easygoing when it came to arrangements concerning the children in the hope that Juliet would always allow him to see the kids when it suited him as his schedule was often inflexible, but Juliet had arranged this visit so the least she could have done was make sure the children were there. 'You could have phoned me, I would have come later. I'm leaving on a training exercise tomorrow, there're a thousand things I've got to do still.' He'd told her that already, which was why they'd made plans for him to see the children today because tomorrow he wouldn't be in Sydney. He'd be sailing north and would be gone for six weeks.

'I know,' Juliet replied. 'But there's something I needed to talk to you about and I didn't want the children to hear so I asked Maggie to take them out.'

'Why didn't you tell me on the phone?'

'I wasn't quite sure what to say. I thought it would be easier just to leave it all until we were face to face.'

She'd met someone. That was the first thought that ran through Sam's mind. The idea made him feel slightly nauseous. While he knew that was probably inevitable, he'd avoided ever thinking seriously about that possibility and he certainly hadn't expected to be forced to deal with it so soon.

Juliet sat down at the kitchen table, motioning for him to do the same. 'I have to go into hospital for surgery.'

Sam let out the breath he'd been holding. That announcement hadn't been what he'd expected and he felt a strange sense of relief. 'Right… good.'

'Good? What do you mean by "good"?' Juliet's tone was incredulous.

'If you're having surgery then I assume that whatever is wrong can be fixed,' he explained. 'That's got to be good.' Yes, he thought, surgery sounded better to him than the alternative—that she'd found herself a boyfriend. That was much better than having to be pleased for her about her ability to move on with her life without him. Surgery he could deal with, he could help, he could be useful. He could do something to assist her. 'What do you need me to do? Do you want me to have the children for a few days?' Excellent. He was able to be easygoing, relaxed and generous, he thought as he offered his help. There was no need for any ill-will. He just hoped she wasn't booked in too soon, and that it could wait a few weeks until he was home again.

'It's a bit more complicated than that. The whole process is going to take a bit longer than a few days,' Juliet said.

That didn't make sense—what surgery took longer than a few days?

Juliet seemed to be able to follow his train of thought. Not surprising really, she knew him better than anyone. 'Surgery is just the first step. I'll have to have some follow-up treatment afterwards and I'm not sure how I'll manage with that,' she explained.

Treatment, not rehabilitation. Sam's relieved state disappeared with that one word. Ongoing treatment didn't sound quite so good.

'What sort of treatment?' he asked.

Juliet's eyes were fixed on his, locked and un-wavering. 'Chemotherapy.'

'Chemo? But…' Chemo meant cancer, that couldn't be right. The nausea was back.

But Juliet was nodding. 'I have breast cancer.'

'Bloody hell.' Now what? Sam was a man; he liked fixing things but he was completely out of his depth with cancer. He needed some details, some facts. There had to be something he could do, something to make him feel useful. 'Are you sure it's cancer? You've had other lumps and they've always been fine—why is this one different? Do you think you should get a second opinion?'

'I've seen my GP and two oncologists, I've had blood tests, a mammogram and a biopsy.' Juliet was reeling off words as if she was reading a shopping list, and Sam was having trouble following her. 'I've had plenty of opinions and they all agree. I have cancer.'

Most of the words made no sense to him. It was as though Juliet was speaking a foreign language. All he really heard was 'cancer'. What was he supposed to say now? What was he supposed to do? He searched for the right words, something, anything to show that she could depend on him, but it was hard to offer support when he had minimal understanding of what was going on. 'So what happens now?'

'I'm booked in for a mastectomy in ten days.'

Ten days—in ten days he'd be on a ship in the Timor Sea.

'Mastectomy?' He knew what that word meant. 'You're having the whole breast removed? Can't they just remove the tumour?' Surely, with all the advances modern medicine had made, that should be possible. Or was the tumour too big?

'One option was to just remove the lump but I tested positive for an abnormal gene, which increases my risk of developing more tumours in the breast tissue. I'm choosing to have all my breast tissue removed to decrease the risk. I don't want to give the cancer any chances to come back.'

She sounded very matter-of-fact but he was struggling to process all the information. 'What do you mean, "all your breast tissue"?'

'I'm having a double mastectomy.'

'Double?' Had he heard her correctly? 'Both of them?' he clarified.

Her breasts had always been large, a CC cup, which on Juliet's tiny frame had always been noticeable, and Sam couldn't imagine her without breasts. He didn't want to imagine her that way.

Juliet nodded. 'I want the odds in my favour. This is the best option. I'll start chemotherapy after the surgery.'

Things were going from bad to worse. He couldn't believe that just ten minutes ago he'd thought that Juliet having surgery was a better option than Juliet announcing she had a boyfriend. Now he desperately wished her news had been that minor. In reality he could have dealt with a boyfriend—one way or another. He was completely out of his depth with this announcement but he was determined to get a handle on the situation and do whatever she needed.

'If the doctors are taking all your breast tissue, why do you need chemo as well?'

'There's always a chance of tumours developing in the small amount of breast tissue that may remain behind after the surgery. The oncologist recommends chemo for pre-menopausal women with this type of tumour,' Juliet said with a shrug of her shoulders. 'It decreases the chance of anything further developing. If he's recommending it, I'm going to follow his advice.'

Sam took a deep breath, trying to organise his thoughts, trying to work out what he could do, how he could help. 'So what exactly does all this involve? What do you need me to do?'

'I'll be in hospital for a few days with the surgery. I'm having that done in the school holidays and I'm going to ask Mum and Dad to have the children. You'll be away.'

As usual. He could imagine Juliet wanting to add the accusation to the end of her sentence. He knew he was away a lot but she'd married a naval officer; he knew they'd had a plan but he'd tried a desk job and he'd hated it. In his opinion he'd done what he could to save their marriage and it hadn't worked. They were both to blame but now wasn't the time to look back. They needed to focus on the present. They couldn't change the past. Their marriage was over and he should be able to travel without feeling guilty, but he knew now that he wouldn't be able to. Not when

Juliet was sick and his children were going to
need him.

In the circumstances he decided it was best to
ignore her comment. He didn't want to start an
argument, especially one he wouldn't win because she was right. He would be away. But he
wouldn't always be away and if he knew what
the schedule was he should be able to be around
for Juliet and the children at least some of the
time. 'And then what?'

'Then I have chemo.'

'How does that work?' It was strange—cancer was such a common disease, everyone knew
someone who'd been affected by it and everyone
bandied around terms like chemotherapy and
radiotherapy, but Sam really had no idea what
any of it meant or how it worked. How exactly
did the doctors target the cancer cells and what
else got damaged along the way? How sick was
Juliet going to get? Would she be in hospital for
weeks at a time? Would she be able to manage
the children? 'Chemo is what you see people
having in the movies when they're hooked up to
the drips?' he asked, needing clarification. He
needed to make sure he understood.

Juliet nodded. 'It's not always given that way but Hollywood makes it look like that. Some of the drugs are given intravenously and others are in a tablet form—it depends what combination the medical oncologist decides to use. Whichever way I have the drugs, the usual process is four lots of chemo given about three weeks apart. The doctors expect me to be finished by Christmas.'

Christmas. Could this be her last Christmas? That thought burst into Sam's head before he could censor it. He couldn't think like that, he knew he needed to stay positive. Juliet needed support, not negativity. He'd stick to getting the facts first, deal with the things that were certainties. 'And how long does each session take? Do you stay in hospital each time?'

What would happen to their children?

'I'll have to go into hospital for a half-day on the first day of each cycle. Then I wait a few weeks and repeat the process.'

'What about the kids? Will you be able to manage them?'

Juliet shrugged. 'I hope so. It's a bit of a waiting game to see how I cope with the chemo. It affects people differently. I might have to call in some favours from friends but if I get really sick I'm sure Mum will come down to Melbourne.'

'You haven't told your parents yet?' Juliet's wording implied she hadn't given them the news.

'Maggie's going to drive us down to Bowral to-morrow. Maggie knows.' Juliet shrugged. 'She'll help me tell Mum and Dad.'

'And what about the kids? What have you told them?'

'Nothing yet.'

Sam frowned. 'What am I supposed to say to them?' He was used to Juliet telling him what to do when it came to organising their family. He was comfortable being in charge on board a naval vessel but when it came to working out domestic matters, he relied heavily on Juliet. As a single father he knew he'd have to work things out for himself, but he hadn't had to deal with anything this dramatic and he was at a loss.

'Nothing. I'll tell them over the weekend when we're at my parents'. Just take them out to dinner, that's what they're expecting. They won't pick up on anything if you behave normally.'

Behave normally! Hell, his wife—ex-wife— announces she has breast cancer and he's supposed to behave normally.

'Sam, I know this is a shock but there's a really good success rate with this treatment regime. I am going to beat this.'

'How can you be so certain?'

'I'm going to have everything that's recommended for me, I will do everything possible, and I'm counting on that being enough. I will do whatever needs to be done and that includes fighting this thing with every bit of strength in me. I am not leaving my children.'

And there it was, the thought that was on both their minds, out in the open. What was going to happen to their family—what was left of it? Even though the children seemed to be coping well with the divorce, he couldn't imagine how they were all going to get through Juliet's treatment, let alone what would happen if she didn't make it. How would the children cope? He knew what it was like to grow up without a mother and it wasn't something he would wish on anyone, especially not his own children.

Juliet knew what he was thinking. 'I understand

that the idea of something happening to me, and what that would mean to the children, worries you. It was the first thing I thought of too. But your mum was killed in an accident—there was nothing that could be done to change that. I can be treated and that's why I need you to stay strong. I'm going to make sure the children are okay through this and the rest of my energy I'll use to fight this thing. I can't be worrying about how the adults are coping. I'm going to fight this and I'm going to win.'

Sam knew Juliet never said anything she didn't mean. She was tiny but so full of courage and determination. He knew she would fight with every last breath and, knowing Juliet, she would win.

Their conversation was interrupted when Maggie arrived home with the children in tow. Sam felt as though his heart would burst with love and pride for his kids but there was also a trace of fear and worry in there too. What would become of them all?

He tried to focus on the children but his mind kept drifting back to Juliet's health. He was still finding it hard to believe they were divorced but the fact that they were made it more difficult now—he would do anything and everything he could to help but how much help would Juliet accept, and realistically, what would he be able to do? He was about to spend six weeks at sea, something that was a regular occurrence and the very thing that had been at the root of their separation. He didn't even know when he'd next have a chance to speak to Juliet properly. Discussing things on the phone hadn't proved very satisfactory in the past and he didn't imagine it would be any easier now.

But she'd need help now. She'd need him.

No, he thought, she had her sister and her parents. Yes, she'd need help but she didn't necessarily need him. Her family was close, they would help her, he had no doubt about that. He was probably a long way down her list and that thought bothered him considerably. He wanted to be able to offer her support, wanted her to be able to rely on him, but realistically it wasn't going to happen. Not when he was going to be out of the country.

He took the children to the Sydney fish markets and the fresh, salty air helped to ease his fears slightly. Being near the sea always made him feel better. He'd missed it when he'd lived in Canberra and he'd missed it when he'd taken leave from the navy to try to save his marriage. He knew now that he needed to be near the ocean, he needed to know that he could get out on the water if necessary. The ocean helped to clear his mind and soothe his soul. He just wished he and Juliet had been able to work out how to have it all, but they hadn't made it.

He and the children walked around the pier before they went to choose their dinner. Dozens of boats were moored to the bollards and Edward had to inspect several of them as they bobbed gently on the waves. Watching Ed, Sam wondered if the love of the sea was a genetic trait. He had it, his father had it, and it looked as though Ed had the same fascination. The scene must have reminded Edward of Sam's father, a retired naval officer who still spent the majority of his time on his own boat, fishing, pottering about or just thinking.

'When are we going to visit Grandad?' Ed asked.

Sam wasn't sure how to answer that. He and

Juliet had made tentative arrangements for the Christmas holidays. This was to be their first official Christmas apart; even last year when they'd been separated they'd still celebrated Christmas together, but this year would be different. Their plan had been that Juliet would spend Christmas with the kids and her folks and then meet Sam in Merimbula, on the New South Wales coast, where the children would spend a week with him and his dad while Juliet returned to Melbourne. Sam had no idea whether that would still be possible. But the kids knew nothing of Juliet's illness yet so he supposed explanations weren't necessary. As far as he could work out, those plans wouldn't need to change.

'I'm going to take you to see him after Christmas. We'll have a holiday at the beach.'

Sam still loved spending time with his dad. Sam was an only child and his mother had died when he'd been about Kate's age—which was partly why Juliet's news had freaked him out—and he'd been brought up by his dad and his dad's widowed sister. They'd been a close family, as close as it was possible to be when his dad spent weeks at sea, just like he himself now did.

Sam knew what it was like to have an absent father but he didn't feel that it had affected their relationship. They were close and they had their shared love of the sea to bond them.

Sam still felt that Juliet had never really understood that the ocean was in their blood and he couldn't stand the thought of not being able to get out on the water. He imagined he'd be like his father when he retired and still spend his time mucking about in boats. He wanted to start teaching the kids to sail and he'd planned to get a little boat this Christmas that they could play around in and keep at his father's. Sam had fond memories of lazy summer days of his childhood spent on the water, learning to sail, and he wanted to create the same memories for his own children. He didn't want these plans to change. Somehow, they'd have to get to Merimbula.

CHAPTER FIVE

September 2008

SAM couldn't settle. He paced in his cabin, unable to relax, unable to keep focussed. He was almost wishing for an emergency. Wishing for something to happen that would distract him from his thoughts. He needed a crisis to demand his full attention because at the moment he had too much time on his hands. Too much time for thinking.

He'd been at sea for nine days with another thirty-three to go.

And Juliet was having surgery. Today.

He'd tried to be positive about the procedure, had tried to tell himself everything would be fine, but day by day the tension had slowly increased until he was edgy and stressed. He hated this feeling of helplessness, hated being so far away. He was starting to understand why Juliet had wanted to keep them all together. He wanted to be with his family too. For the first time in a long time he didn't want to be at sea—he wanted to be in Melbourne.

He left his cabin, unable to endure its confines a minute longer. Maybe the ocean breeze would clear his mind and settle his nerves. It usually did.

He nodded to the few sailors he passed on his way to the deck but didn't stop to engage in conversation. His mind was too preoccupied to discuss anything more detailed than the weather, but the fresh air didn't allay his fears. His thoughts followed him, colliding with each other inside his head just like the waves he could see crashing into the bow of the ship as he stood at the rail. All the different scenarios rolled through his mind, threatening to overwhelm him. What if the surgery was unsuccessful? What if Juliet didn't even make it through the surgery? What if he lost Juliet not through divorce but through death?

He hadn't considered the divorce to be a final, complete separation. He knew they'd always be connected through their children but the idea of losing Juliet altogether was devastating. The thought had been in the back of his mind since she'd told him about her diagnosis—had that really only been ten days ago?—but he'd managed to suppress it until now. Until she was undergoing surgery and he could no longer ignore just how serious this situation was.

He'd arranged for flowers to be delivered to her at the hospital. It had seemed important to him to let her know she was in his thoughts but now his thoughts were far from sunny and light, nothing like the flowers he'd sent. Now that seemed like such a minor, meaningless gesture. What good would flowers be?

He closed his eyes and let the salt spray fall on his face. There had to be more he could do. Juliet deserved more.

He should be there. He should be with his wife.

That thought confirmed his dilemma. He still thought of himself as married. He still thought of Juliet as his wife. She was still his responsibility and he should be by her side. But instead of being there and supporting her, he was thousands of miles away in the middle of the ocean.

Juliet had been right. He had his priorities wrong. He'd made the wrong choice.

He felt helpless. Devastated. Lost.

Would he have a chance to fix things?

Juliet sat on the hospital bed with her back to the doorway. It wasn't the door she was afraid to face but the mirror beside it.

'Are you okay? You're very quiet.' Maggie was standing behind her, brushing her hair like she'd done years ago when they had been children.

Juliet nodded. Maggie's strokes were long and rhythmical, almost hypnotic, and Juliet's mind drifted as her hair was tended. She wasn't okay, far from it, but she didn't really want to tell her sister where her mind had drifted to—she had a feeling talking would make the situation worse, not better.

'Shall I plait it for you?' Maggie asked. 'You'll have to wear one of those paper hats in Theatre— tying your hair up will keep it under control.'

Juliet knew she'd be going off for surgery soon and as the time approached she found herself becoming increasingly nervous. The surgery itself didn't bother her and she'd made the decision to undergo surgery without hesitation. In her opinion surgery was her only option, but what if it wasn't enough? What if the cancer was lurking somewhere else in her body? What if she couldn't beat this?

Juliet could feel Maggie lift the weight of her hair in her hands, separating its length into three strands before twisting them together. Her chestnut hair was long and healthy—it had always been one of her features that she'd liked and she'd looked after it. So far her hair looked like it always had if she ignored the odd grey hair— it was still glossy and thick. The rest of her also looked the same as she'd done for the past twenty years, give or take a few wrinkles. So far the only things about her that had changed were all on the inside but still she'd become wary of mirrors. She was wary of confronting her physical self. She knew she was trying to forget what she looked like so the new Juliet wouldn't be so much of a shock.

Today was the beginning of some major changes. And some big losses. She knew very well that her hair might not be with her for much longer but she also knew she could live without it. She was going to lose much more than her hair. Just as long as she didn't lose her life. As long as she could live she didn't care about her hair. Or any other parts of her.

'Did Mum ring this morning?' Maggie's question interrupted her ponderings.

Juliet nodded.

'How did she sound?'

Juliet had been dreading telling her parents about her cancer. She'd been far more nervous about giving her parents the news than she had been about telling Maggie and Sam. How did a daughter tell her parents she had a malignant tumour? What parent wanted to be told their child might die? But having Maggie's support when she'd made the trip to see them had helped immeasurably. And Juliet had been surprised at how well they'd taken the news.

Her mother had been shocked initially. Juliet had seen the shock roll across Harriet's face as she'd processed the news. She'd seen her try to compose herself, try to hide her thoughts, but she'd always been easy to read. But Harriet recovered well and started doing what she did best—organising her family. It was her way of holding things together.

Her parents had listened as Juliet had given them the information she'd had and then they'd taken over, planning the logistics of having their grandchildren to stay and organising support for Juliet. Juliet had wished her mother could tell her everything would be okay but she knew that wasn't possible. She knew her mum was waiting for someone to tell her the same thing but all Juliet had been able to do was give her the facts—she couldn't make any promises. But just sharing the information with two more people, two people who she knew would do anything for her, had eased her anxiety.

Telling her parents had been difficult but now that they knew she felt the burden had lifted. As always, her parents had the ability to make her feel better about the situation. Part of her wished she could ask them to come down to Melbourne with her but Kate and Edward would be better off in Bowral. They would benefit from John and Harriet's reassurance and Juliet really didn't want to expose her children firsthand to the events of the next few weeks. It would be much better for them to stay protected up there until she knew how things were going.

'I think she'd like to be here,' Juliet answered, knowing that was how her mum felt, even if she hadn't voiced that opinion. 'But I really couldn't cope with lots of people around,' she added honestly.

'Is that why you asked Mum and Dad to have your kids?'

'Partly. You know how Mum is. She's much better if she's busy, and looking after the kids will keep her occupied, give her less time to worry.'

Maggie nodded in silent agreement. 'How were the kids?'

'Good. They've been yabbying and looking after the chooks and bottle-feeding the lamb the neighbours gave Dad.' She could picture the two of them, running amok around the farmhouse and the few acres that her parents had on the outskirts of Bowral. They would be enjoying their country holiday with their grandparents, oblivious to what was happening in Melbourne, and that was the way she wanted it. 'I think they've got plenty to occupy them and it's far better to have them busy up there.'

'What did you end up telling them about your surgery?' Maggie asked as she finished plaiting one half of Juliet's hair and started on the other side.

Juliet had found it difficult to know what to tell the children. She'd been worried about imparting more bad news so soon after the divorce and she'd discussed her concerns with Maggie.

'I was vague. Sam and I spoke to a child psychologist before we told the children about the divorce and she suggested that we tell them only what we thought they needed to know. She said to give them enough information so they could make sense of what was happening without overloading them. I thought that was good advice and something that would work in this situation too.

'I didn't think they needed to hear about the worst-case scenario,' she continued. 'I know they'll realise I look different so I've prepared them for that. I told them I found a lump in my breast and the doctor is going to take it out to make sure the lump doesn't grow. They know to expect my breasts to be smaller. I couldn't quite tell them they'd be gone altogether and I haven't mentioned chemo yet or the word *cancer*. I wasn't sure how much they would understand. I can give them more information as I go through the treatment.'

'I think they'll surprise you with how well they cope, especially if how they've dealt with the divorce is any indication,' Maggie responded, showing her support for Juliet's decision.

Their conversation was interrupted at this point by the nurse who bustled into the room and dropped a gown on the bed beside Juliet. 'Can you change into this for me? You'll be going to Theatre soon.' She barely paused to make eye contact before she hurried out again, saying she'd be back shortly.

Maggie snapped an elastic band around the tail of Juliet's plait. 'I'm finished. Do you want me to wait outside while you get changed?'

Juliet shook her head. 'I need to use the bathroom,' she said. It wouldn't have mattered any-way—she'd been stripped naked and poked and prodded in front of more people than she cared to think about over the past six weeks so undressing in front of her sister was no big deal.

She picked up the gown and went into the en suite bathroom. She stripped off her T-shirt and bra. Out of habit her fingers went to her left breast, palpating the lump. She wasn't sure when that had become a habit. Just as she wasn't sure if she was still hoping that one day, miraculously, the lump would have disappeared. But there it was. It was the size of a walnut in a shell but she knew that a few months earlier it had been the size of a pea.

The diagnosis had put her into a spin—the divorce had turned her life upside down but getting the diagnosis of breast cancer had sucked her into a vortex and the only way to stop her life from spiralling out of control had been to fight. And she was fighting with everything she had, starting with sacrificing her breasts. She was going to fight this disease and she'd keep fighting for as long as it took to beat it. That was the only way.

Today was step one. The mastectomy.

Her heart rate increased at the thought of it.

I am not scared, she told herself.

She wasn't afraid of losing her breasts. Her breasts were insignificant, inconsequential. They were nothing compared to her children. She wasn't prepared to leave her children without a mother, and if that meant letting someone take her breasts, it was a small price to pay. She'd chosen surgery without hesitation and once she made up her mind she very rarely changed it.

Saying she wasn't scared of the surgery itself was probably an understatement. She wasn't afraid of having parts of her removed. She didn't think she'd miss her breasts and she didn't imagine anyone else would either, but she was a little apprehensive about the risks associated with surgery. She had to get through it. Her children needed her.

Juliet turned her back to the bathroom mirror as she slid her arms into the gown and fastened the tie behind her neck. But avoiding mirrors didn't completely mean she could avoid her reflection. As she emerged from the bathroom she could see Maggie waiting for her. She knew how similar they were so she was still able to picture herself in Maggie's image. Maggie, older by four years, was taller and slimmer but their colouring was identical. Juliet always thought of herself as a rounder version of Maggie. Even now, with the weight loss she'd suffered, that was still the case. In their younger years Maggie had always complained of being too skinny and had called Juliet 'curvy'. She'd been envious of Juliet's bust but, as was the way of teenagers, Juliet would have happily swapped her CC cup for Maggie's narrow hips. Maggie had an oval face and Juliet's heart-shaped face also made her seem slightly rounder by comparison. But while their physical shape was different, their identical colouring always identified them as sisters. They had the same chestnut hair, although Maggie's had a wave in it while Juliet's was heavy and straight, the same bright blue eyes, the same fair skin with a dusting of freckles across their noses.

Looking at Maggie now gave Juliet a teensy insight into what her body might look like after surgery—without the narrow hips. She had decided not to have a breast reconstruction immediately and she knew it would be strange not to feel top heavy, but she could cope with looking like her sister—at least until she decided what to do about new boobs.

'I brought you a present,' Maggie said as she handed Juliet a small, flat parcel. 'I'll make sure it's beside your bed when you wake up—it'll help to remind you that you're doing the right thing.'

Juliet unwrapped the gift. It was a photo of her children that had been taken at their grandparents' house on the weekend that Juliet had visited to tell them the news. Kate and Edward had been feeding the lamb and smiling up at the camera. They had been full of life and their sheer delight had been captured perfectly. Maggie was right, the children were the reason she was here. They were everything.

'It's perfect, thank you.'

Maggie hugged her just as the nurse came into the room to take Juliet to Theatre. 'It'll all be fine,' Maggie said as she kissed Juliet's cheek before putting the photograph on the bedside cabinet for her.

Juliet was wheeled off to Theatre still thinking about her children. They had taken the news of her surgery remarkably well considering they were probably still processing the reality of the divorce. Or perhaps she was projecting thoughts onto them. She liked to think that she'd told them as much as they needed to hear, but was it possible they were coping so well because they were still too young to really understand everything that was happening? So far the divorce hadn't really affected their day-to-day lives and they didn't know anyone who'd had major surgery so the idea of something going wrong would not occur to them. Cancer was also an alien concept to them and one Juliet was not about to mention at this stage.

She had explained the operation in very simple terms but she guessed that until they saw the post-op result, until they saw her in her altered state, the surgery wouldn't mean much. The rest of the treatment—the chemotherapy and any reconstructive surgery—she would explain later. One thing at a time, she'd decided. There was no point telling them about things that would happen months down the track—that was far too distant in their future.

She had reached the Theatre suites now and had been transferred to the operating table. The surgeon was in the room and she'd been connected to monitors. The anaesthetist had begun.

The anaesthetic had been administered and the mask had been placed over her face. Juliet was counting down now. This was it.

Fourteen weeks to Christmas.

Thirteen years she'd known Sam.

Twelve weeks of chemo.

Eleven…

Juliet stirred. She was vaguely aware of being in a strange environment but what she was most aware of was pain. She was flat on her back and her chest was on fire.

'Juliet.' Someone was leaning over her, leaning into her field of vision. 'The surgery is all over, and you're in Recovery.'

She remembered now. The mastectomy.

'Have you got any pain?' The person leaning over her was a nurse. It hurt just to breathe and Juliet didn't dare move. Was the nurse serious? Of course she had pain. She tried nodding her head.

That was a mistake. Just that slight movement intensified the pain and she felt a wave of nausea wash over her. She must have looked as bad as she felt because the nurse reached behind the bed and grabbed a small green bowl. Juliet turned her head just in time, wincing as the pain carved through her chest, and vomited into the bowl.

It didn't help. She felt as though her chest was being split open, ripped apart along the seam that turning her head had created. The nurse waited until she'd finished then gave her something for pain and nausea, but the cycle continued for several hours. She vomited at regular intervals and she couldn't work out whether pain was making her vomit or whether the vomiting was giving her pain.

The consensus was she had reacted badly to the anaesthetic and that had caused the nausea, which had exacerbated the pain. Eventually the nursing staff got everything under control but by that stage Juliet was so exhausted she felt she could sleep for days. As the pain receded she sank blissfully into a state of oblivion.

Juliet opened her eyes and cautiously looked around the room. She saw that she was out of the critical care ward and back in a private room, but she had no idea how long she'd been there. She'd been vaguely aware of people coming and going around her bed but she'd lost track of the days. She remembered seeing Maggie but couldn't remember whether that was a before- or after-surgery memory. She supposed it didn't really matter what day it was, although she'd ask the first person she saw just to satisfy her own curiosity.

The first person to come into her room was one of the nurses, bringing a delivery of flowers. 'Aren't these gorgeous? Someone's thinking of you,' the nurse said as she handed Juliet the blooms. 'I'll just go and find a vase.'

Juliet held the flowers. Yellow tulips. They were her favourites. She knew who they were from without reading the card that was nestled in their midst.

Sam.

'What is the date?' she asked the nurse, before she could disappear from the room. It wasn't idle curiosity making her ask the question but a sixth sense suddenly telling her it was now important to know what day it was.

The nurse paused in the doorway. 'September the twelfth.'

'Oh.' Juliet slipped the card from the little

plastic stick and opened it. It was hand-written in Sam's neat, precise script. That surprised her. She thought he would have just dictated a message over the phone to the florist.

My darling wife,
I hope you are recovering well and that these tulips bring a bit of sunshine to your day.
I will see you soon, all my love, Sam.

Juliet read the card again. *My darling wife*—did Sam have difficulty remembering they were divorced too? Nearly three months after signing the papers Juliet still thought of herself as married. When would that change?

They would always be connected but at some point, surely, she'd have to accept that she was single.

Accepting it wasn't the issue. In her head she knew she was divorced but in her heart she still felt married.

Had Sam's wording been deliberate? Had he used the word *wife* on purpose? Juliet could remember exactly where she'd been thirteen years ago today. Did Sam remember too? She counted the tulips—thirteen. He hadn't forgotten either.

Whenever Juliet saw a yellow tulip she was instantly transported back to Canberra in spring of 2005. Sam had taken her to the Floriade flower festival on the shores of Lake Burley Griffin. She closed her eyes as she let her mind drift back.

It had been a glorious September day, with the sun shining in a cobalt-blue sky. The water on the lake had been unusually calm and everything about the world had seemed right. She'd been able to smell freshly mown grass and popcorn as they'd waited in line for the Ferris wheel, standing among some of the thousands of spring blooms that were specially planted for the festival. Hundreds of visitors had wandered through the acres of gardens but Juliet had only been aware of Sam. They'd boarded the Ferris wheel and when their carriage had reached the summit it had come to a stop. Looking down, Juliet had seen a carpet of yellow tulips spread our beneath them, blanketing the ground like a reflection of the sun. It was such a happy colour and it had suited her mood perfectly. Sam, however, had been more interested in looking at Juliet.

September the twelfth was the day he'd first told her he loved her, cuddled together on a seat at the top of a Ferris wheel. And on September the twelfth, thirteen years ago, above a sea of yellow tulips, Sam had proposed. Today was the anniversary of their engagement.

But thirteen years later everything had changed. The fairy-tale had unravelled. Juliet opened her eyes. Her dreams lay shattered at her feet in a million tiny pieces and her heart sat heavily in her chest, a leaden weight, immobile, stitched inside her skin.

Her body had failed. Her marriage had failed. She felt betrayed. Despite the tulips there was no gallant knight on a noble steed coming to rescue her.

The twelfth of September was now the anniversary of her surgery. It was no longer a celebration.

The mild perfume of the tulips suddenly made Juliet nauseous and she thrust them to the end of the bed just as the nurse returned with the vase. Juliet was about to ask her to take the flowers away but she hesitated, not quite able to part with them. The nurse picked them up, arranging them in the vase before placing it on the bedside table. Juliet turned her head, watching the nurse's movements, and her gaze settled on the photograph of her children that Maggie had given her.

She would keep the flowers, she decided. Her marriage might be over but she still had a lot to be grateful for. She was going to concentrate on saving her future. Her children's future. September the twelfth would be the anniversary of the beginning of the rest of her life. There was nothing to be gained by rehashing the past. The fairy-tale might be over but if she was lucky, her life wouldn't be. She had vowed to fight and she wasn't finished yet. Other battles had already been lost and she wasn't going to lose this next one.

The nurse picked up Juliet's chart. 'Do you need anything for pain?' she asked.

The pain of the surgery was bearable now, as long as she didn't move too much, and the nausea had settled almost completely, but Juliet's heart was hurting. She needed to rest and she wanted to sleep so she asked for the medication that was due.

Perhaps she shouldn't have because when she did drift off to sleep it wasn't restful. Whether it was the medication, the after-effects of the anaesthetic or just circumstances Juliet didn't know, but whatever it was it resulted in a dream that was far too realistic for her liking.

She was walking along the coast. She could feel the breeze in her hair, could smell the salty tang of the ocean, but she didn't recognise the beach. She did, however, recognise the figure walking a few hundred metres in front of her. It was Sam. He was wearing shorts and the green polo shirt he'd worn the night he'd taken the children to dinner at Sofia's, the night of their divorce. Where were they? And why were they there?

She called his name, hoping the wind would carry it to him. He turned. He'd heard her. He was smiling and Juliet's heart flipped in her chest, just like it did every time Sam's right-to-left smile lit up his face. He held out his arms, open and welcoming, and Juliet felt the last vestige of pain in her chest float away. But before she could move, before she could take another step towards him, Kate and Edward appeared from behind her and ran into Sam's embrace.

He hadn't been looking at her, she realised. His smile hadn't been for her, it had been for his children.

Sam waited for the children and then turned and kept walking, holding their hands. No one paid Juliet any attention. It was as though she was invisible.

Juliet was frozen to the spot, unable to move, as she watched her family walk away without her, without so much as a backward glance. They continued walking along the beach, every step taking them farther away from her. Didn't they know she was there or did they not care?

Just as Juliet thought she couldn't feel worse, she saw an unfamiliar woman walking up from the water's edge to join her family. The woman entered the tableau from the side so Juliet couldn't see her face, only her back. Juliet called out but if anyone heard her this time, no one turned around. No one stopped. She was helpless, immobile, trapped in a nightmare, and there was nothing she could do as the woman walked away with Sam, Kate and Edward. Her family.

It didn't matter that Juliet couldn't see the woman's face, she knew who she was. She was her replacement.

She woke with a start. She must have moved as she'd woken up because her chest was burning. The dream was so real, so vivid, and Juliet knew she wouldn't forget it easily.

She lay still in bed, waiting for the searing pain in her chest to subside as she thought about the dream. What did it mean? Had Sam remarried? Replaced her?

She'd been able to see everything. Had she been able to hear them? Had they been able to hear her? It didn't appear so. A horrible thought hit her. Was the Juliet in the dream dead?

Would Sam want to give their children another mother? Someone who bought him green T-shirts that matched his eyes. Someone to plait Kate's hair just as she did now. Someone to cook pancakes for Edward.

Juliet had always been so terrified of Sam going off to war and getting himself killed. She'd been terrified of becoming a widow like Maggie. But what if she was the one who died?

She hadn't really wanted a divorce but her

pride and stubbornness had led her down that path before she'd realised where she was heading, until all of a sudden there had been no turning back. Part of her still thought they could salvage the situation. If they couldn't, she knew they would make the best of the hand they'd been dealt, but what if she wasn't even around? She didn't want her children to need another mother. She didn't want someone else taking her place.

She wanted her kids to know she loved them. She wanted that to mean something.

She lay in her hospital bed, physically and emotionally bruised. The truth of the matter was that she loved her kids and she still loved Sam.

What a fool she'd been. How much damage had she done? Could she fix things? Thoughts whirled around in her head, colliding with each other, confusing her.

Should she try to mend things or was it just circumstances making her feel melancholy? Had there been an opportunity to save their marriage? Had they really tried as hard as they could have?

She shook her head in a physical attempt to stop the mental battering her thoughts were giving

her. When they'd separated she had been ada-
mant they'd done their best. She couldn't afford
to have doubts now.

The fairy-tale was over. End of story.

2007

Juliet had told people that she and Sam couldn't
agree on where to live, couldn't agree on what
was best for the children, but it was more than
just a disagreement over location. But she'd never
spoken the whole truth to anyone.

They had left Darwin in 2000 and moved to
Sydney. That had suited Juliet perfectly as she'd
been close to Maggie who was still recovering
from her husband's death. Kate had been born
that year and Edward two years later. Life had
been good for their little family.

In 2003 Sam had been transferred to Melbourne.
That move had also been easy but they had begun
discussing what they would do once the children
started school. Juliet didn't want to move them
every three years for ever—she didn't think it
was fair. Sam had said it hadn't bothered him
when he was growing up as a defence force kid
but Juliet didn't want to point out that, after his

mother had died when he had been just seven, he'd been dealing with bigger issues than moving house.

She also knew that while Edward would cope with frequent moves, Kate, with her more serious and introverted personality, probably would not. She wanted Kate to have time to settle into school and make friends. She didn't want to be uprooting her every few years.

At the end of 2005 they were looking at another transfer, this time to Adelaide. It was defence force policy to move their people every three years. This transfer didn't constitute a promotion for Sam, it was just a scheduled transfer and Juliet put her foot down. Kate was about to start school and Juliet wanted her transition to be as smooth as possible. Kate had been diagnosed with suspected dyslexia and Juliet wanted her to start school with her friends from kindergarten, not be moved interstate, as she thought Kate had enough to deal with. They had been working with a tutor and she and Kate had established a good rapport. Juliet wasn't prepared to disrupt that. She refused to move their family, and while she wasn't mean enough to make Sam leave the navy she did want him to explore other options. Sam, to his credit, did try to work with her demands, at least initially. He took a six-month leave of absence from the navy, something the defence force was always happy with. The navy figured it was better to give people leave than to lose them all together. The defence force human resource department even helped to find Sam a civilian position through their contacts. In this instance being magnanimous worked out perfectly for the navy—they looked like the good guys and within six months they had their officer back.

The job they found for Sam was with an oil company that had drilling operations in Bass Strait, south of Melbourne. It sounded ideal but the only problem was that he didn't get to go out to the oil rigs, he didn't get to go out to sea, he didn't get to fly in choppers. He was a desk jockey. His work was operational trouble-shooting and he was good at that. He'd had plenty of experience in planning, scheduling and problem solving, but there wasn't enough variety or physical work to engage him. He missed the danger and excitement of the navy.

He was bored. Bored and unhappy. He missed the ocean and he missed the diversity. While he loved routine in his home life, he discovered he hated it in his job. He was miserable at work and he brought that home with him.

He joined the country fire service, a volunteer emergency services organisation, looking for something to satisfy his need for adrenaline bursts. Endless meetings and training exercises took over his weekends and weeknights, not to mention the actual emergencies that took him away from the family too. Bushfires, storm damage, flooding, trees falling onto houses and across roads all seemed to need the services of the CFS. And Sam was always available. He needed the excitement.

To Juliet it seemed as though Sam was home even less than before. He couldn't get his fix of adrenaline from his work or his family and he got more and more involved in the CFS. His need for excitement and danger and the ever-decreasing time he spent with his family made Juliet suspect he was punishing her deliberately and she grew resentful and bitter. She couldn't believe he needed to spend so much of his time with the CFS and she started picking arguments. She could hear the accusations in her voice but she couldn't seem to stop herself. Their conversations became terse until they almost stopped conversing altogether. Eventually Juliet realised this life was never going to be exciting enough for Sam.

At the end of Sam's leave of absence he was offered a six-month secondment to Singapore on a training mission. The family could go with him and he thought that was a perfect solution.

'I'm not prepared to move the children every three years—what makes you think moving every six months is any better?' Juliet argued.

'We can stay together this way,' Sam countered. 'If I was going off to combat, you couldn't come too. Isn't this better?'

'If you were going to war, we wouldn't have to move anywhere.' At that stage Juliet thought that sounded like the better option and the thought horrified her. She'd always been terrified that Sam would be sent to a war zone and never come back, and now she was thinking that was a better scenario. She must be mad.

'I've accepted the position.'

'You're going? We're not discussing this?' Sam had taken it without consulting her? 'I have given up everything to follow you—my home, my career—and you know why I can't keep doing this. If it was just me, that would be different, but this affects our children too. I can't believe you would do this to them.'

'I think you're being melodramatic. I haven't gone into this blindly. The schools are world class. Kate will be fine.'

'Melodramatic!' Sam hadn't been listening to anything she'd said. 'You want to move us to Singapore for six months and then what? Where will we be six months after that?'

'I can't tell you that.'

'Because you don't know, do you? It's all in the hands of the defence force.' It was obvious to her then that they needed a break. 'I'm not going to let the navy dictate our lives any more.'

Sam had a different opinion. He left for Singapore. Juliet knew he was eager to get back to navy life and that thought hurt her more than anything. She so badly wanted to be enough for him. Wanted their family to be enough, and she thought, hoped, that when he returned to the navy he'd realise he missed them, realise he was missing the opportunity to watch his children grow up. In Juliet's mind it was a trial separation and she accepted that, confident that Sam would eventually return to them.

But things turned out differently.

The six months in Singapore was extended to twelve and, in hindsight, Juliet realised she should have gone with him, but she'd made such a big deal about keeping the children settled she couldn't then back down. Once again her stubbornness and pride got in the way. Her mother used to say that pride came before a fall, and she was soon to find that was true.

At the end of the year Juliet wanted him home. She filed for divorce, thinking it would make Sam realise what was important, but that backfired spectacularly. Sam chose the navy over his family.

That was her interpretation. Juliet knew Sam saw things differently.

CHAPTER SIX

October 2008, a Friday

JULIET was nervous. Her palms were clammy, she could feel every beat of her heart pulsing in her throat and her stomach was in knots. Her second round of chemo started today, she was due at the hospital in an hour, but that wasn't causing her nervousness.

Sam was back from his six-week exercise in the Timor Sea. He was flying into Melbourne this morning. He was coming to spend a weekend with the children and they were going to a beach house on the coast, but when he'd found out she had an appointment he'd offered to take her to the hospital. He was due to arrive at her house in fifteen minutes and she was getting herself into a right state.

He hadn't seen her since the surgery.

He hadn't seen her flat-chested.

He hadn't seen her since her hair had started falling out.

Juliet was scared of his reaction. She didn't expect him to vocalise his thoughts but she was terrified that she'd be able to see them reflected in his eyes. She was afraid she'd see herself reflected there and she was fearful of what that might look like.

Her own reaction had frightened her at first and she thought she'd been prepared. For twenty-three years she'd been an hourglass shape and suddenly she was a pear, all hips and no breasts. Her tops hung loosely on her frame, making it obvious, in her mind, that something was missing, almost accentuating her new shape. She hadn't done anything about buying special bras yet, ones that would give her a false profile because she hadn't thought it was a priority and her chest was still too sore to contemplate the idea of wearing anything firm against it. But now, with Sam's visit looming, vanity was getting the better of her. She didn't want to look different, not to him.

She stood in front of her wardrobe, wrapped in the comforting warmth of her old dressing-gown, as she tried to find something to wear. She grabbed a black shirt dress. She didn't want to wear anything figure hugging—that would only make things worse—and slipped her arms into the dress, fastening the buttons. The shape was okay but it made her look like she was going to a funeral. Not the look she was after. She took it off and threw it on the bed. She continued to rummage through her clothes, searching for something that made her feel confident.

The pile of discarded clothes on her bed grew higher. Sam would be there in five minutes. The next thing she found would have to do. She gave up looking through the clothes on hangers and searched the drawers. She found a light woollen top in a navy, grey and white argyle pattern. She grabbed it from the pile, hoping the pattern would cover a multitude of sins, pulled on jeans and a T-shirt and dragged the jumper over her head.

She glanced quickly in the mirror, still not completely comfortable with confronting her own image. The top wasn't a bad choice as the pattern did camouflage her flat chest to some degree. Anyway, it would have to do, she was out of time.

She cleaned her teeth and ran a brush over her hair, trying to ignore the strands of hair that clogged the bristles. In the last week her hair had started to fall out. Not enough that anyone looking at her would notice, but she was finding hair on her pillow in the morning, in the shower and in her brush. She consoled herself with the thought that at least the chemo was targeting cells and she just hoped it was getting the cancer cells too.

There was a knock on the door. Juliet took a deep breath. She'd had four weeks to get used to her new look and she still found it confronting. How was Sam going to react?

He wasn't sure what he'd been expecting to find when he saw Juliet. He'd expected her to look different but he wasn't exactly sure what changes might have occurred. He'd prepared himself to be surprised, shocked even, but she looked just the same. Her chestnut hair was still long and thick, framing her heart-shaped face. Her blue eyes were enormous in her pale face and her freckles were perhaps more prominent against her skin, but otherwise she still looked like his Juliet. She was still beautiful.

He stepped through the door and bent down to hug her. His greeting was automatic and it was then that he felt the difference, felt the change. She was skin and bone, the comforting softness of her breasts gone.

Juliet sucked in a breath, short and sharp, as he hugged her.

'I'm sorry, Jules, did I hurt you? I wasn't thinking.' Had he hurt her? He couldn't believe he'd been so careless—being hugged was probably the last thing she wanted.

She shook her head as she pulled out of his embrace. 'I'm fine,' she said, but he noticed she avoided eye contact. What didn't she want him to see?

'We'd better go. Parking might be hard to find.' She turned round to grab her car keys from the hall table and Sam could see the change now. Juliet's familiar profile had been replaced by one he didn't recognise. The familiar swell of her breasts had disappeared and in their place was nothing. He'd known what a double mastectomy meant yet he still hadn't pictured the reality. Hadn't been able to imagine it. And now he didn't need to imagine any more; he could clearly see just what this cancer had done to Juliet. He had felt it and he'd seen it.

He tried to hide his surprise as she turned back and handed him the car keys. He hadn't expected such a dramatic change. And if the physical changes were so obvious, what about the emotional strain? How was she coping with that? He knew surgery had been her choice but were the changes worse than she had expected too? How was she managing on her own? Maggie was back in Sydney and Juliet was responsible for the normal family routine again. Was it too much for her? Did she need more support? He didn't really understand what was involved with regard to her treatment. He knew that the lymph nodes that were excised during the mastectomy had tested negative for cancer cells and that her first dose of chemo had gone smoothly, but he wasn't up to speed on the process of chemo or the potential side-effects. How much of an effect did the chemo have on her physical capacity?

Sam knew he had to do something, had to offer

some kind of support, but he hadn't been able to work out what to do or how to do it. He didn't know what Juliet needed or what she'd accept. He needed more information about what she was going through and how she was coping, starting with what happened today. He took the opportunity to ask questions as he drove her into the hospital.

'Do you see the surgeon today?' he asked as they waited at a red light at the corner of Swan Street and Punt Road.

'No. Dr Benson is the surgical oncologist, I've finished with him.' She paused. 'Hopefully. The medical oncologist is in charge of the chemo. That's Dr Davey.'

Sam had looked at various websites, trying to find information about chemotherapy, and he tried to recall what he'd read. He didn't suppose it mattered to him which doctor was which, he just wanted to know what they were going to do for, and to, Juliet. 'What does he do exactly?'

'One of the first things they'll do today is take some blood. It gets tested and once the test results come back, Dr Davey will see me and review my treatment.'

'What are they testing it for?'

'To see if my white blood cell count is okay. If it's too low, it lowers my resistance to infection and they'll send me home and give me some more time for my count to build up. But I've been feeling okay so hopefully I'll get my second dose. I don't want any delays, I want to get this all finished before Christmas.'

'Would you like me to come in with you? Keep you company?' he asked as he navigated the right-hand turn into Punt Road.

'I'll be at the hospital for the best part of four hours. You don't want to sit there all that time, do you?'

'I've got no commitments until Kate and Edward finish school and kindy.'

She didn't answer immediately. Would she rather be alone?

In his imagination Sam could picture Juliet sitting in a room full of strangers, everyone hooked up to various machines and monitors, all looking tired and ill. Juliet looked well—if he could ignore the fact she'd lost her curves. She was still gorgeous and he couldn't imagine her sitting alone in a group of sick people. He didn't *want* her to sit there alone. He wanted to be with her.

Should he have told her that? He wasn't sure. He didn't know if she would have felt obliged to let him accompany her and, as much as he wanted to go with her, he didn't want to put her in a situation that made her feel uncomfortable. He tried a different explanation. 'I'd like to understand your treatment—if the kids ask me questions about what's happening it'd help me if I've seen what goes on and it would help to clarify things for me.' He flashed her a smile. He knew how she felt about his smile and he just hoped that hadn't changed. He knew he wasn't playing fair, using the children in his bargaining, and hopefully using his smile to his advantage, but he wasn't sending her in there alone.

She shrugged and nodded. 'If you're sure,' was all she said in reply. Sam took that to mean yes.

Juliet directed him to the most convenient parking garage and then led him to the oncology unit. She was signed in and once the nurse collected her it was a slow but steady process through a battery of tests. Juliet introduced him to the nurse as her 'support person'. He noticed her slight hesitation before she clarified his position and he wondered what she'd been about to call him. He wasn't sure what he wanted to be but he supposed 'support person' was probably the best he could hope for at the moment.

Juliet's blood pressure, pulse rate, temperature, height and weight, even her respiratory rate were all recorded before her blood was taken and finally a bung was inserted into her elbow ready for the IV attachment. They were then sent back out to the waiting area.

'What happens now?' he asked.

'We wait. Once Dr Davey has reviewed my test results, I'll see him. There's a lot of sitting around.' Juliet pulled a book out of her handbag. 'Why don't you grab something to read from that magazine rack?' She indicated a stack of magazines and newspapers on the opposite side of the room. There wasn't anything else to do; they could hardly have a private conversation in a room full of people, so Sam perused the selection and chose something to flick through while they waited.

He'd read the same article three times by the

time Juliet was finally ushered through to see Dr Davey.

Once again Juliet introduced him as her support person but this time Sam wasn't so surprised. If that description meant he got to sit in on all her consults, it was fine with him.

Dr Davey shuffled some papers on his desk. 'Your blood tests are all okay,' he said once they were all seated. 'I assume since I didn't hear anything after your first dose of chemo that you didn't have any adverse reactions?'

Juliet shook her head. 'No major problems at all.'

'No nausea, no constipation?' Dr Davey clarified.

'I kept my fluids up and everything was fine.'

'Well, we can start the second dose today. I'll increase the dosage slightly and same rules apply—if you experience any problems, make sure you let the clinic know. Do you have any concerns at all before we begin?'

Sam waited for Juliet to speak first but she just said everything was fine. She might understand what was going on but Sam had lots of questions.

But no one seemed to expect him to say any-thing—no one looked in his direction or gave him an opportunity to talk. Before he realised what was happening Juliet was standing, waiting for him to join her. Dr Davey wrote in Juliet's notes and saw them to the door. The appointment was over. It was all rather anti-climactic in Sam's opinion, done and dusted before he'd absorbed what had been discussed.

One of the nurses took Juliet's case notes and led them to a large room, which Sam would have called a ward except there were no beds. In the spots where he assumed the hospital beds would normally be were recliner chairs. It reminded him of a day surgery recovery area. Some of the chairs had the curtains drawn around them, others were in full view. Some were occupied and some were empty. The people in the chairs—the patients, he supposed—were all hooked up to drips. Some were sleeping, some were chatting, others were reading. He was surprised to see how relaxed everyone seemed.

Sam pulled an armchair up next to Juliet's re-cliner as a second nurse joined their little group. The two nurses double-checked Juliet's name, cross-checking it with the hospital name tag around her wrist, and then double-checked the medication order with the medications on the tray. Apparently everything was in order because Juliet was handed a tablet and then the nurse hung a bag on the dripstand and connected Juliet to it.

Juliet washed the tablet down with a drink of water before explaining what was happening. 'The Adriamycin is given through the drip. It blocks DNA production and kills cells. The tablet was Cytoxan. It stops cells from dividing so basically it stops new cancer cells growing. The Adriamycin won't kill all the cells in one go so if the doctors can stop cell division as well then the number of cancer cells will gradually decrease and there will be fewer cells to be killed each time. Does that make sense?'

Nothing about this made sense to Sam but as long as the combination of surgery and chemotherapy worked, he didn't care if everyone but him spoke Swahili. As long as they cured Juliet.

Juliet had chosen a chair at the far end of the room and at this stage the neighbouring chairs were all unoccupied. The medication could take a couple of hours to run through the drip and Sam was grateful to be away from the other patients, out of earshot. He needed to discuss some things with Juliet and didn't want the whole room to hear.

'How have the kids been coping with everything that's been happening? Is there anything I need to know before I collect them this afternoon?'

'Ed's doing fine. Nothing much worries him and I don't think he's really noticed any change to his day to day life. Kate's a little more clingy than usual. She's been fine until this past week. My hair has started to fall out and I think that's freaked her out a bit.'

Sam found himself giving Juliet's hair a closer look, it looked like it always had to him, thick and dark and glossy. 'Your hair doesn't look any different.'

'There's been quite a lot of hair on my pillow in the mornings. I've been trying to clean up the evidence before she sees it but she's been coming in to my room during the night so it's not always possible to hide the fact that I'm losing my hair,' she explained.

Sam knew a common side effect of chemo was hair loss but he had no idea to what extent it could be expected. 'Are you likely to lose all your hair? Is it going to cause problems for Kate, do you think?'

'The Cytoxan is causing the hair loss and it's quite likely I'll lose it all.' She shrugged. 'I'm telling myself that at least it means the drug is having an effect but I'll need to be conscious of Kate's reaction. I might need a wig. I have the number of a cosmetician and I'll make an appointment to see her. I think it would be a good idea if I can try and minimise, or at least disguise, some of the physical changes. It might lessen the trauma for the kids.'

Sam found the idea of Juliet losing all her hair quite disturbing. If that was his reaction, he could imagine how Kate might feel.

'I'm sure she'll be fine with you,' Juliet continued, 'but just expect her to stick a bit closer to you than normal. The weekend at the beach might be just what she needs. It might give her a chance to feel as though everything is fine.'

Juliet had read his expression, misinterpreting it slightly. Sam didn't correct her, choosing to follow her line of thought instead. 'You think that's still a good idea, the beach? You don't want us closer to home? What if you need someone?'

'I'll be fine, and Gabby and Finn are only a street away if I need something. I haven't had a lot of energy lately so it'll be good for the kids to have some fun.'

'Do you think they might want another beach holiday over Christmas?'

Juliet looked startled by his question. 'Why?'

'Edward was asking when he was going to see my dad. I sort of promised that we'd go to Merimbula after Christmas. I've taken leave and I thought a week at the beach would be nice.'

'You want to take them for a week?' Juliet's expression was flat and Sam wondered what the problem was.

'It was what we'd planned, remember?'

'I know, but a week's a long time.'

Sam frowned. 'It's not really,' he argued. 'I thought it might give you a chance to have some peace and quiet, some recovery time. I know you were going to go back to Melbourne but you could stay with your parents instead, have some time out.'

'I don't think I want time out and I don't want to be separated from the children for a whole week. That's too long.'

'You want me to take them for a shorter time?' Sam was a reasonable man but he wasn't about to miss out on time with his children.

'I'm not sure,' she replied.

'I have a better idea.' Another plan came to him suddenly and he wondered why he hadn't thought of it earlier. 'Why don't I drive up to Bowral on Boxing Day and collect you all.'

'You're inviting me too?'

Sam nodded. 'You can have your R&R in Merimbula. It might not be as peaceful as staying at your parents' but this way we can both have time with the kids. Dad and Aunt Helen would be thrilled—they'd love to see you as well.'

'Can I have some time to think about what I'll do and let you know? Maybe I could come at the end of the week for a few days.'

'You decide and let me know but it's no problem for you to stay the whole week if you like.'

He hoped she'd see the sense in joining them. The sunshine and fresh sea air would be a perfect tonic but he recognised that now was not the time to make an issue with it. He didn't want to be overbearing. He'd sown the seed of the idea and he hoped Juliet would agree to his whole plan.

The drip had run through and the nurse arrived to disconnect Juliet. She took a final set of obs before announcing that Juliet could go home. Sam waited while she went through the discharge summary with Juliet, explaining the anti-nausea medication to her and instructing her to drink plenty of fluids.

Watching Juliet being poked and prodded, seeing her being dwarfed in that huge recliner chair looking so tiny, fragile and pale, had brought out his protective instincts and he knew that he wasn't averse to the idea of her joining them in Merimbula. She needed looking after, that was obvious, and it would be so easy to look after her if she was by his side. If he could convince her that the ocean air would do her good then he knew, with the help of his dad and his Aunt Helen, they would be able to restore some of her spirit. The more he thought about his suggestion, the more he liked it. He'd keep working on her—it was in everyone's best interests for her to agree.

By the time Sam had driven Juliet home he had just enough time to gather the children's bags before leaving to collect them from school. He'd wanted to head straight to the beach, hoping to get out of the city before the weekend peak-hour traffic started, but he wasn't totally comfortable with leaving Juliet alone. Only after making her promise she'd call if she had any problems did he finally get into the car, but he was still uneasy. He checked in on her every hour for the rest of the day and first thing on Saturday morning. Each time Juliet insisted she was fine but it was only when she told him to stop bugging her and to enjoy his time with the children instead that he finally stopped checking up on her and did as he was told and relaxed and had fun with his kids.

October 2008, a Sunday

The setting sun was low in the sky and the clouds looked like tufts of pink cotton candy against a honey background as Sam turned the hire car into Juliet's driveway. He and the children had had a busy two days at the beach, body-surfing, playing beach cricket and collecting shells, and now Kate and Edward were both asleep in the back seat.

Sam left the children in the car. He'd get Juliet to open the door and then he could carry them straight to bed. He'd rented the cottage until tomorrow to give him a full day's access today, which had given him time to bathe and feed the children before returning to Melbourne. He'd wanted to make things easy for Juliet. It was something he could do and he was pleased with his planning. He knocked on the front door and was surprised when his knock went unanswered. He'd sent Juliet a text message telling her what time to expect them and he'd thought she'd be waiting at the door, eager to see her babies. He knocked again and tried the front door. It was locked and there was no sound from inside.

His bewilderment turned to concern. He pulled his phone out of his pocket, checking for messages. Juliet hadn't replied to his text. Was she out or had something happened? It was out of character for her not to keep in contact.

He stepped off the veranda and skirted the house. He stood on the rubbish bin and peered through the garage window. Her car was there. He tried the back door but it was also locked. He dialled the home phone number as he reached into the spot where they'd always hidden the spare key. Old habits die hard, he thought as he retrieved the key. He could hear the phone ringing inside, his call going unanswered. He didn't hesitate any further but slipped the key into the lock and opened the door.

The house was dark and quiet. 'Jules, we're home—are you here?' Sam stepped into the family room. This room and the adjacent kitchen were both empty and silent. His worry increased. 'Jules?' he called as he continued up the passage.

A noise made him glance to his right. Something moved on the bathroom floor. It took his brain a moment to process the picture. Legs and feet were just visible through the bathroom doorway.

'Juliet!'

Had she collapsed? He took two steps and was in the bathroom. Juliet was lying on the bathroom floor, her head cushioned on a bunched-up bath towel.

How long had she been lying there? Was she conscious? He could smell vomit. Was she breathing?

He squatted down beside her and put his hand on her wrist, feeling for a pulse. He felt it, weak and rapid. He touched her forehead. It was cool, no sign of a temperature. He moved his hand to her arm. That was cool too—shouldn't she be warmer?

'Jules? It's Sam. Can you hear me?'

She opened her eyes when he spoke and lifted her head at his touch. She attempted to sit up.

'Wait. Don't try to sit up. Tell me what happened first.'

'Nothing happened. I'm just sick.'

Why was she lying on the bathroom floor? 'You promised you'd call. Have you been vomiting all weekend?'

'No.' She shook her head weakly. 'Only this afternoon.'

Sitting up must have disagreed with her. She

leant over the toilet bowl as she retched. Sam gathered Juliet's hair into a ponytail and held it away from her face as she heaved, but there was nothing in her stomach to bring up. He waited for the convulsions to stop before he let go of her hair. Dark strands of hair clung to his fingers. He shook his hand and the strands fell to the floor, gathering in clumps on the white tiles. He tried to block the picture from his mind. 'Tell me what I can do, Jules. What do you need? Shall I get those tablets the doctor gave you for nausea?'

Juliet shook her head. 'I've tried taking those but I just vomit them straight back up. Nothing's staying down.'

'There must be something we can do. Let me help you into bed and then I'll call the doctor. You can't stay lying here.'

He scooped her up in his arms, ignoring her protests and her assurances that she was capable of walking. If she was capable of walking, why had she been lying on the cold, hard bathroom floor? She was light and fragile in his arms and all his protective instincts rushed to the fore. He would sort this out for her, he would make sure she was okay, he wasn't going to leave her on her own in this condition despite her protests.

'Where are the kids?' she asked as he laid her down on her bed.

'They're asleep in the car. I'll bring them inside in a minute. They're okay for now. Let's get you sorted.' He fetched a bucket from the laundry and a clean towel from the bathroom. Juliet's dark hair was littering the bathroom floor, stark against the white tiles. He swept it up, removing all traces of it, conscious of Kate's potential reaction to the sight, and then brought the children in from the car. Once his family was all in bed he turned his mind to Juliet's predicament. He needed some advice; he had no idea what to do. He looked up the phone number for St Vincent's Hospital, hoping to find a twenty-four-hour helpline for the oncology department, but the best he could do was the emergency department. He was quite prepared to drive her to the hospital and he wouldn't hesitate to phone Gabby and ask her to come and mind the children, but the nurse who answered the phone suggested that he call a locum. That sounded like good advice to Sam, only he didn't know if Juliet's GP used a locum service. The nurse passed on a number and Sam was gradually able to get the situation under some semblance of control.

The locum doctor gave Juliet two injections, an anti-emetic for nausea and a sedative. 'That should settle things down for her,' he explained. 'Get her to take the anti-nausea tablets tomorrow but if she still can't keep anything down, you'll need to take her in to the hospital.'

By the time Sam had paid for the service and seen the doctor out, Juliet was asleep. Sam was relieved. Juliet needed to rest but his mind was whirling. He couldn't believe he'd found her prostrate on the bathroom floor. Alone. Why hadn't she called him? Why hadn't she called someone? What if she'd been home with the children? Would she have called someone then?

He hoped Juliet would have reacted differently if the children had been home. He was almost certain she would have—the kids were certainly the first thing she'd thought of when he'd arrived back; she didn't want them to see her in that state any more than he did. He had to assume she would have called somebody if she'd been home alone, even if it was only to take the children out of the house.

The questions that had been plaguing him for weeks ran through his mind. Was there anything he could do? Or should do? How many decisions could he make? How much input could he have? What did Juliet need? What would she accept? For weeks he'd had no answers but suddenly he realised what he needed to do.

He'd worry about the Christmas holidays and their trip to Merimbula later. Juliet needed help now and he would give it. He wouldn't wait until December, he would stay by her side right now. She wouldn't be able to argue with him as it was in the best interests of their children. He just needed to organise it.

CHAPTER SEVEN

JULIET slept solidly for twelve hours and woke early, feeling much better. She rolled onto her side and came face to face with Sam. The surprise made her gasp and whether it was that small sound or her movement it was enough to wake him.

He stirred and opened his eyes. His face was only inches from hers. The slightest movement would bring him within reach. Without thinking, she stretched out one hand and her fingers brushed his chest. She was disoriented for a moment, lost in the past, their past.

He wasn't wearing a shirt and his skin was warm and lightly tanned. His green eyes darkened with her touch and, suddenly realising what she'd done, she quickly withdrew her hand.

'Good morning. How are you feeling?' His voice was husky, thick with sleep. Juliet's skin tingled as a shiver of longing ran through her, reminding her again of the years before.

'Much better,' she replied as she fought to regain her equilibrium. Those years were over. They would now only be a memory. 'Have you been here all night?'

'Pretty much.'

'Oh.' Her stomach did a strange, slow, belly-flop. Sam had been lying beside her, close enough to touch, all night.

'I was worried about leaving you on your own in case you were sick again.'

Any romantic notions she'd been harbouring were quickly dispelled.

'Are you hungry? Can I make you some toast?' He was all business.

Sam loved a project. A mission. Fixing things, problem solving was what he did best, and Juliet knew he saw her as a project. Something that needed sorting out, but she was fine. She didn't want to be seen as a problem that needed solving.

'I'm fine. You don't need to stay. Haven't you got a plane to catch?'

'I've changed my flight. The locum said to

make sure you could keep something in your stomach today and I'm going to follow his advice. I'll leave when I'm sure you're okay.'

Even though she didn't want to feel like a charity case, she was grateful for Sam's concern. Despite saying she was fine she really didn't want to be alone after her experience yesterday and she wasn't convinced that she was one hundred per cent better.

'Toast sounds good, then, thanks,' she said, accepting his offer of help.

'No problem. You stay in bed and I'll bring it to you. I'll make breakfast for the kids too.'

The children! Were they awake? Had they seen Sam lying beside her? 'Have the kids been in?' Her heart was in her throat as she asked the question. She didn't want to have to explain the picture to the children.

'No. They're still sleeping but I don't expect that will last much longer.'

Sam rolled out of bed and stood and stretched. His back was to her and he was wearing only a pair of shorts. She let her eyes run over him, taking in his broad shoulders and lean trunk. She could see the muscles flexing over his shoulder blades as he stretched his arms, and she watched them ripple and move as he lowered his arms to his sides. He was a picture of health and Juliet was well aware of the contrast between his peak physical condition and her own. Any remaining fantasies she'd been harbouring about the night in a shared bed were now completely obliterated. She rolled onto her side as Sam left the room, turning her face away from the door.

She heard Edward getting up a few minutes later. As usual he went straight to the kitchen, always ready to eat the minute he woke up. Kate surfaced shortly after and Juliet lay in bed, expecting her to come into the room, as was her normal habit, but she bypassed Juliet. Had she been lured by the sound of Sam's and Edward's voices coming from the kitchen? Juliet lay in bed, alone, trying to decipher the muted strains of conversation.

Eventually the conversation came to her when Sam and the children brought her breakfast.

'Kate, can you get ready for school?' Sam said as Kate put a plate of toast beside Juliet. 'I'll drop you off this morning. And do you think you can help Ed find some clothes too? I want to talk to Mummy.'

Kate nodded but Juliet started to protest. 'I'll get up and help get them ready.'

'Kate can manage, can't you, sweetheart?' Sam interjected.

Juliet was about to argue before she realised that Sam was right. Kate was perfectly capable of doing the task and would probably enjoy the responsibility. She needed to let the children help in whatever ways they could.

She picked up her cup of tea as her children left the room. 'What did you want to talk to me about?' she asked Sam.

'I've got a proposition for you.' He sat on the edge of her bed. He looked worried. His forehead was furrowed and there were creases in the corners of his green eyes. 'You frightened me last night.' He sounded worried too and his concern made Juliet feel better. Just knowing he cared helped. 'What would have happened if I hadn't come back when I did? What would have happened if you'd been home by yourself with the children? Would you have called someone?' Oops, now he sounded annoyed.

'Of course I would,' she retorted. Defending a hypothetical situation made no sense but he seemed to expect an answer.

'Who would you have rung?'

'Gabby or Anna. I told you Gabby and Finn were in town—they would be happy to help.'

'They have their own families. Do you think it's fair to rely on them?'

'They've offered to help and I know they mean it. I'd do the same for them. What exactly are you getting at?' She knew he was building up to something, she could see it in his expression.

'I don't think you can cope on your own with the kids—'

'I've managed often enough on my own with the children,' Juliet interrupted. She was cross now. There had been plenty of times when Sam hadn't been around to help and she'd managed perfectly well. She couldn't believe he was going to criticise her now.

'Jules, let me finish.' Sam's demeanour was calm, in contrast to her rising temper. 'I was going to say "just while you're going through chemo". I was on the internet last night, researching the drugs you're taking. Dr Davey increased the medication this time. What do you think will happen next time if you have a similar reaction?'

She shrugged. 'I don't know.' How was anyone to know? 'I'll speak to Dr Davey and see what he suggests. Okay?'

'I have a better idea. Why don't I take the children to Sydney to look after them there while you finish your treatment?'

'No. Absolutely not.'

'I didn't think you'd like that option. Which leaves option two. I will take leave until Christmas and move down to Melbourne to help you.'

Sam sounded as though the decision had been already made. Juliet wondered what his agenda was. 'Why?'

'Because I can.'

Juliet didn't respond. She just looked at him, waiting for him to elaborate. At this point it didn't sound like much of a reason.

Sam continued. 'I want to help. You're the mother of my children. We may be divorced but I still care about you and about how you're coping. I can run around after the children, take you to your appointments, do the cooking. It would make things easier for you if you had help.'

'I can pay for a housekeeper,' she retorted. '*You* can pay for a housekeeper if it makes you feel better. You don't need to take leave. I don't need full-time help.' As much as she'd appreciated his offer of help when it was for the day, the idea of having Sam around for the next few weeks was unsettling. She didn't want him to think she couldn't manage. She didn't want to think he might be right.

'But I can do it. I want to do it. Think of it this way if you prefer—wouldn't this arrangement be better for Kate and Edward too?'

'You'll take leave? Just like that?'

'I've been in the navy for twenty years. I think I'm owed some carer's leave.'

'I'm not sure it'll work.'

'It will. Tell you what, if I can prove to you how easy it will be, if I can organise leave by the end of the day, will you let me stay and help?'

'You want to stay here?'

Sam shook his head. 'I think that's a bit too confusing for everyone. I'll find something close by. A short-stay apartment should do.'

She knew she should argue, knew she should insist that she could manage, but the reality was that she could use the help and the kids would benefit from having Sam around. But it was only a temporary solution so would it make things more difficult in the long run? She wasn't sure and she really had no way of knowing.

Juliet stayed in bed and ate her breakfast as Sam got the children ready for school. Her mind was buzzing but eventually she decided that, until Sam had made firm arrangements, she didn't need to worry about hypothetical situations.

She waited until Sam had left to drop the children off before getting out of bed. She had intended to have a shower but a wave of dizziness threatened to overwhelm her, and sitting on the edge of the bath to clean her teeth was all she could manage before collapsing back into bed. She wouldn't refuse Sam's help, she decided, even if it was just for the day.

Sam came into her room when he got home. He had a bag laden with fresh fruit and vegetables in one hand and a paper bag from the pharmacy in the other. He handed the paper bag to Juliet.

Inside was an assortment of vitamin supplements. 'What are these for?' she asked.

'I rang Dr Davey to get his advice. He suggested you continue with the anti-nausea tablets and also take these. If you're not starting to feel better in another twenty-four hours, he wants to see you. Did you manage to keep breakfast down?'

She nodded.

'I've got some phone calls I need to make but why don't I run you a bath first?'

A bath had sounded appealing until Juliet faced the reality of her naked figure. She knew she'd lost weight but when she was dressed she could ignore the bony protuberances. Now the harsh morning light was exaggerating every angle in her normally curvaceous figure. Even her thighs were thin and floppy she noticed as she stepped into the bath. Her skin, although normally pale, had an unhealthy tinge of yellow and her chest was disfigured by scars.

Juliet slid quickly under the water, letting the bubbles hide her nakedness. She thought she looked ten years older and she felt it too. She closed her eyes, trying to picture something other than her flaws. All she could see behind her closed eyelids was Sam's smile. In her mind she turned him round and feasted her eyes on his naked back as she remembered how he'd looked when he'd climbed out of her bed that morning. He was perfect, his tanned, toned muscles contrasting dramatically with her own pasty, flabby flesh.

Tears rolled from the corners of her eyes. She shouldn't care about how she looked. She should only care that she was alive but she couldn't stop crying. Being alive wasn't enough for her today. All she could think about was what she'd lost. Emotionally and physically.

She knew she was being pathetic, wallowing in self-pity, but she couldn't stop.

She sank under the water, letting her tears mingle with the bathwater. She stayed submerged until she ran out of air. Rising to the surface to breathe, she concentrated on filling her lungs. She wiped her face, removing the traces of tears and water, and climbed from the bath. She hurriedly towelled herself dry, keeping her back to the mirror.

When Sam came to check on her she was back

in bed and she'd stopped crying, but she knew her eyes were still puffy and red.

'What's wrong?' he asked.

'Nothing,' she replied, trying to look as if she had her emotions under control. 'I'm just having a moment.'

'Are you feeling sick?' he asked as he placed another cup of tea on her bedside table, next to the bottles of supplements.

'No, I'm feeling like a failure.'

'What do you mean?'

'I thought I'd cope better than this. I had no problems with the first lot of chemo and I expected the same outcome this time, but you're right. I can't manage to look after the children like this. I can't even manage to look after myself.'

'That's why I'm here. It's my turn to look after my family. Think of all those times when I was away and the burden of responsibility fell on you—it's my turn now.'

'And what if I don't beat this? What then?'

'You will.'

'How can you be so sure?'

'Because you told me so yourself.' Sam's face

lit up as he smiled at her. His green eyes were shining and his smile lifted Juliet's spirits a little. 'I know you—I know how stubborn and determined you are. You can do this but there's no reason to do it alone. Let us help you. Let *me* help you.'

She'd been trying so hard to keep things together, telling everyone she was going to beat this cancer, but even she wasn't convinced it was true. She knew that Sam's presence would ease the pressure on her—that was why she'd dissolved into tears in the first place, because suddenly she wouldn't have to be the one who was making sure things ran smoothly. She wouldn't have to be the one who worried about whether or not the children had clean uniforms and fresh food for their lunches. She wouldn't have to worry about ballet lessons and play dates. Sam's offer was terribly tempting and she didn't have the energy to refuse. 'Can you stay?' she asked. While the idea of Sam seeing her in a weakened, unattractive state was daunting, she did find the idea of having someone to share the burden appealing.

'Do you want me to?'

She nodded. If he was offering to help, she was

going to accept it. Hopefully he'd seen her at her worst last night and she'd worry about the ramifications of having him back in her life later.

'Good, because I've organised leave. If everything goes according to plan, you have eight more weeks of treatment and I have eight weeks of leave. We're sorted. I just need to find some accommodation close by.'

A wave of relief rolled over her. Could she push her luck a little bit further? 'About that…' Juliet hesitated. 'It would be easier if you stayed here, with us, if you're here to help.'

'Probably, but it's okay. I'll find something.'

'Why don't you make up the spare bed in the study? That would be the sensible option, wouldn't it?' If Sam was there in the morning, she wouldn't have to make sure she was up before the children, up in time to clean up any hair that had fallen out during the night before Kate saw it. It would be easier for everyone if Sam was close to hand, wouldn't it?

Sam wasn't sure if staying in the house was the best option. Did he want to be a guest in his old house? Would he feel like an intruder? But he had offered his help, and he'd been prepared to insist that Juliet accept his help so her suggestion was probably not worth arguing over. Juliet obviously wasn't well enough to look after the children and they were his responsibility. Staying in the house would make things easier, so he accepted with good grace and prepared to get on with caring for his family.

For the next two weeks he ferried the children around, shopped for groceries and cooked. Luckily the children were happy to exist on meals of pasta and barbecued sausages, but he was worried about Juliet. She was so thin and so pale and so tired. For the first week he was there she spent most of each day in bed. That was good; it was what she needed, but what bothered Sam was that he didn't have to insist that she rest. She didn't want to get up and that wasn't like the Juliet he knew. She would get out of bed in the afternoon when everyone was home but he could see the effort she was making and how taxing it was for her to pretend to the children that everything was fine. They ate dinner together as a family, although Juliet barely ate, existing on fruit and mashed vegetables.

By the middle of the second week things were improving. Juliet started to feel better in herself and Sam was relieved. While he understood the effects of the chemo he had struggled to come to terms with how harsh it was and the physical changes in Juliet were confronting. It was hard to watch the woman he loved suffer. He had done everything he could to ease the burden but it was a huge relief when she felt like getting out of bed again. When he got home from dropping the children at school one morning he was thrilled to find her showered and dressed and tidying the kitchen. He handed her a card that Gabby had given him that day at the kindergarten.

'What's this?'

'Gabby has invited us to dinner for her birthday.'

'Both of us?'

He nodded.

'What did you tell her?'

'I said I would pass it on to you.'

Juliet glanced at the invitation before dropping it onto the kitchen bench without comment.

Her lack of interest surprised him. 'What do you think?' he asked.

She shrugged.

He hadn't realised how much he'd been looking forward to going out with Juliet but perhaps she didn't want to go with him. 'Would you rather go on your own?'

'No, it's not that. I just don't feel up to going out.'

'I thought you were feeling better.'

'I am but I don't think I'm ready to get dressed up and make witty conversation.'

'These are your friends, Jules. No one is going to expect you to be the life of the party.'

'The death of the party would be more like it.'

'What do you mean by that?'

She turned to face him. 'Look at me.' She raised her hands to her shoulders and swept them in front of her down to her hips. 'I look dreadful.'

'I think you're gorgeous.' She was pale and too thin, a shadow of her former self, but in his eyes she was always beautiful. Her blue eyes were even more striking now, contrasting with the pallor of her skin, and her fragile appearance made him want to scoop her up and protect her from the world.

'And I think you're a terrible liar,' she replied.

But Sam didn't care what Juliet said because she was smiling and she hadn't smiled at him in days. She'd smiled for the children but it had been obvious to him that she'd been making an effort to keep up appearances, but now her smile was natural, unforced, and it was all the reward Sam needed.

'If you don't believe me, can I make a suggestion?' he asked. She looked at him warily, one eyebrow raised. 'Why don't I ring the cosmetician, the one the oncology nurses told you about? She might be able to suggest some things that might make you feel brighter.' He half expected his idea to be shot down in flames but Juliet actually acquiesced and fortunately the cosmetician had a free appointment. Sam wasn't certain that he would have got Juliet there on a different day.

He drove her to the appointment and although she wouldn't let him go in with her she seemed happy enough when he met her afterwards. He hoped the session had gone well. It hadn't oc-curred to him until she'd gone in that it could be too much for her.

'How did you go?'

'Good news and bad news,' she said. 'She showed me some tricks to put some colour back in my face and suggested I get a wig sooner rather than later if I'm planning on wearing one. She said it's better to start wearing it before my hair falls out. There's no point in waiting until it's all gone.'

That was what he'd been worried about. Would the cosmetician be too blunt? Would the conver-sation remind her of how she'd changed or help to boost her confidence?

'Is that what you want to do?' he asked.

'If I can find a wig that doesn't look too fake, I'll wear it. I think it would be better for the kids.'

'Did she tell you where to get one?'

Juliet nodded. 'There's a good wig shop in the city, that's the good news, but clothes are a dif-ferent story. I wanted to get something that put a bit of shape back for me but the best shop is in Canberra. I guess I'll have to try online.'

'Why don't we start with your hair?'

'Now?'

Sam shrugged. He figured he was here to help so he might as well do this, and as Juliet seemed happy to embrace the idea of boosting her appearance he figured they might as well start today. 'Why not now? We've got time. I've always wondered what you'd look like as a red-head,' he said in an attempt to lift the mood.

Juliet tilted her head to one side, a slight frown on her beautiful face. 'Really?'

'Yep.'

'Okay, then.' It was her turn to shrug. 'But I'm not sure about a redhead. Don't blondes have more fun?'

'I don't think I'd be any competition for Marilyn Monroe,' she said half an hour later as she pouted at him from under a curly blonde wig.

'That's not so much Marilyn, more Shirley Temple.'

'Hey, be nice, this was your idea!' Juliet laughed and Sam absorbed the sound. He couldn't re-member when they'd last laughed together. There hadn't been much to laugh about, and it felt good to share this moment. It felt like old times.

'Try this one instead,' he said, handing her a wig of long, straight auburn hair. He was sure the colour would complement her complexion. The blonde made her look washed out and she didn't need that at the moment.

She whipped off the blonde wig and exchanged it for the red.

'The colour's better,' he said, and it was a big improvement, the deep auburn shade a good foil for her pale skin and blue eyes.

'But I look about fourteen.'

He nodded. She was right.

'What about this?' The sales assistant was holding another auburn wig but this one was in a short, cropped style. Juliet's expression was dubious. 'It'll look better on,' the sales girl insisted.

Juliet held out her hand. 'All right, in for a penny, in for a pound,' she said as she swapped wigs.

'Wow.' Juliet looked amazing. Sam felt as though he'd had the wind knocked out of him and he was almost speechless. He would never have guessed a hairstyle could make such a difference but the transformation was incredible.

'You like it?'

'You look sensational.' He'd always liked Juliet's long hair but he had to admit she looked fantastic with this crop. She was small enough to get away with short hair and it suited her heart-shaped face. The sales girl knew her stuff.

'Really? I don't look like a boy?'

Sam shook his head. 'It's perfect.'

'What about the first one I tried on?'

The first wig had been a match to her normal hair in both style and colour. 'That was fine but this one is fantastic. If you're looking for something to give you a confidence boost, this is it.'

'I don't know,' Juliet wavered. 'You don't think this one is too extreme?'

He knew what she was really asking. Wouldn't it be better to look like her old self? Would a drastic makeover be too much for the children, Kate particularly?

'Why don't we get them both?' he suggested.

'What for?'

'So you have time to think it over. Or you can show the kids, see if they have a preference.'

Juliet allowed herself to be persuaded and Sam happily paid for both wigs. If it was going to mean she felt able to face an evening out with her friends, and with him, it was money well spent in his opinion.

Juliet was dressed, eventually. It had taken her ages to choose an outfit because even though dinner wasn't about her, she wanted to look good. She wanted to look healthy. She didn't want the focus to be on her and the better she looked the more people would treat her normally. She'd finally settled on a blue shirt with a ruffled front. She hadn't had time to do anything about her wardrobe but at least this shirt would disguise her flat chest.

Her hands shook as she snapped the back onto her diamond earring. It was only a small group invited to dinner for Gabby's birthday and Juliet knew almost all of them well, yet she was still nervous. She hadn't been out for a while but that wasn't what concerned her. It was the fact that she and Sam were going together.

She adjusted her wig, staring at her reflection

in the mirror. She was ready. She couldn't delay any longer.

Sam was waiting in the family room. 'You look fabulous, Jules.'

His gaze was fixed on her face and he flashed her a smile, his gorgeous right-to-left smile that made her toes curl.

His compliment made her cheeks flush and she touched the wig self-consciously as she paused in the doorway. 'Thanks.' She'd decided to wear the short auburn wig. She knew Sam liked it but it was Kate's influence that had finally persuaded her. 'Kate helped me.'

Kate was hovering near the kitchen bench and he winked at his daughter, making her laugh. 'Good job, Katie.' He turned back to Juliet. 'Are you ready to go?'

'Just let me make sure I've got everything.' Juliet made a show of checking in her handbag, using the time to regain her equilibrium. Sam's compliment had pleased and surprised her and his smile had thrown her further out of kilter. It had seemed more potent than usual or perhaps it was something in his eyes tonight. He looked like he had a secret and she was dying to know what it was.

But if he had a secret, it didn't seem as though it was one he was going to share with her. There was little time for any sort of private conversation. Gabby and Finn were both gregarious and so were many of the other guests. It made for a lively evening and Juliet found she was enjoying herself. People were glad to see her but after asking her how she was feeling they didn't question her at length about her cancer, and she was pleased to find that she was able to forget about it herself for a few hours and just enjoy the company. Particularly Sam's company.

He was very attentive, behaving as if they were a newly dating couple and not ex-husband and wife. She wondered if the others noticed Sam behaving any differently before realising that what she and Sam did was of little consequence to anyone else.

Sam was sitting on Juliet's right and on her left was Gabby's brother, Ben, whom Juliet had met for the first time tonight. She'd seen photos of him. He was one of Melbourne's most eligible bachelors, according to the social pages, and Juliet assumed it was to do with his status as heir to his father's publishing company. It didn't hurt that he was extremely good-looking—tall, dark, handsome and rich—not a bad combination, Juliet thought. She knew nothing about him really and assumed he was single by choice, but her curiosity got the better of her and she decided she needed more information. Gabby's seating arrangements were perfect—sitting next to a stranger meant that Juliet could pretend she was just like everyone else at the party, fit and healthy—without the stigma of cancer hanging over her head.

She was curious to know what Ben did for a living. 'Do you work in publishing, Ben?' she asked.

'No. I'm a doctor.'

'Really?'

'Yes. That surprises you?' He was smiling at her, obviously not offended by her faux pas.

'No. Yes. I—I guess it d-does,' she stammered, a little embarrassed by her mistake. 'Funny how you make assumptions, isn't it? Sorry.'

'Don't apologise. It's a common misconception. But I do wonder why Gabby is allowed to be an

artist but everyone expects me to work in the
family business. Everyone except my parents.'

'What sort of doctor are you?'

'A plastic surgeon.'

'A cosmetic surgeon?'

'A cosmetic surgeon is a Hollywood thing.
Technically I'm a plastic and reconstructive
surgeon but I think plastics has become inter-
changeable with cosmetics in people's minds.'

'What's the difference?'

'Cosmetic surgery is a form of reconstruction
but it's really just elective surgery—for people
who want to change their appearance. Plastics
and reconstructive work grew from a need or
ability to repair deformities that were either con-
genital or following a trauma of some kind.'

Perhaps Gabby's seating arrangement wasn't
accidental—Juliet wasn't sure if she was game
to ask. 'So do you do any cosmetic surgery or
do you only do serious things?'

'It's all serious.' Ben paused slightly. 'Well, it is
to the people undergoing the procedure. Even if I
think it's unnecessary, if my client can convince
me that there's a good reason for the surgery, if it

can be justified, I will consider it, but my passion is reconstruction work.'

'So is there a difference between breast reconstruction and breast augmentation, for example, or is it just semantics?' Juliet couldn't resist asking.

'Technically they are both cosmetic but augmentation is simply changing someone's appearance for the hell of it, whereas reconstruction is repairing, restoring if you like, someone's appearance. Mostly that's done just to make them look like they did before.'

Juliet hadn't really investigated the procedure, it hadn't been a huge priority, but meeting Ben gave her food for thought. She would consider it and if she wanted to look into it further, she now had a place to start. She would get Ben's details from Gabby if she needed them, she decided. A dinner party was probably not the appropriate place for a longer discussion about the ins and outs of breast surgery.

Dessert had been served and it was obvious the other guests were in for a late night, but Juliet was looking pale and, even under her make-up

Sam could see the dark circles beneath her eyes. It was time to go. He thanked Gabby and Finn and bundled Juliet out to the car.

'Have you had a good evening?' Sam asked as he pulled into the driveway.

'It's been lovely but I am looking forward to climbing into bed.'

'Why don't you get ready for bed? I'll sort out the babysitter and bring you a cup of tea,' he offered. 'And you can sleep in tomorrow. I'll take the kids to the park.'

Juliet didn't argue.

Sam carried a cup of tea in one hand and an envelope in the other. Juliet was in bed. She'd taken her make-up off but was still wearing her wig. He put the cup on the bedside table and handed her the envelope.

'What's this?' she asked.

'A surprise. A good one, I hope.'

Juliet smiled. Her face was aglow. The colour of her wig emphasised the blue of her eyes and they sparkled in the dim light. Sam felt a stirring of desire. Despite the circumstances his reaction to her was as potent as ever. She was still the only woman capable of taking his breath away.

Juliet opened the envelope and pulled out the sheets of paper inside. 'Plane flights to Canberra?' She looked up at him, a slightly puzzled expression on her face.

'I thought we could take the kids up there for a weekend. Show them some of our old stomping ground and maybe you could do some shopping.'

'The shop the cosmetician was telling me about?' She guessed his agenda.

Sam nodded. He'd seen how much difference the wigs had made to Juliet's confidence. He wanted her to feel as good as possible and he hoped this shopping trip could help. 'I thought it would be nicer to shop in person instead of online.'

'That's a brilliant idea. The kids will love a weekend away. When did you want to go?'

'I thought we could play it by ear a bit, see how you feel after the next lot of chemo and go then if you're up to it.'

'That sounds like a plan. Thank you.' She grinned and Sam enjoyed the feeling of satisfaction that spread through him.

'My pleasure. Now, drink your tea and get

some sleep.' He kissed her gently on the forehead, savouring the creamy scent of her freshly
washed skin.

He closed the bedroom door softly behind
him.

He was pleased with the outcome. If he could
prove to Juliet how much better things worked
if he was around, how much more smoothly
things ran with them working together, perhaps
she would agree to give him another chance.
Getting her to Canberra and boosting her confidence with an updated, tailor-made wardrobe
would surely serve to further his chances.

He knew he still loved her; he had never
stopped, and being together, even under such
difficult circumstances, had made him question
why he had given in to her before and hadn't
fought against the divorce. She'd applied for it
and he'd never denied her anything if he could
help it. She had convinced him it had been in
the children's best interests but now he doubted
that.

He would be patient but he was going to get
his family back.

But there were a few final hurdles. Baby steps,

that's what they needed. Getting her to Canberra was step one, getting her through chemo was step two and getting her to agree to spend New Year in Merimbula with his side of the family was step three. Little steps to show her how much better things could be if they were together. A family again.

Who knew if there would be more? But if there were, he would get through them all. He wouldn't rest until they were together again.

CHAPTER EIGHT

December 2008

IT WAS early morning on New Year's Eve as Sam and his father headed out to sea, heading towards the rising sun. They travelled in silence, Sam's father steering the boat as he checked his electronic fish finder, searching for decent schools of fish, while Sam prepared the rods and lines. They were both completely at ease on the water and had spent hundreds of hours together fishing and many fewer hours talking.

Sam watched his father as he stood in the cabin. He was concentrating on the job at hand and unaware of Sam's scrutiny. Sam was looking for any signs that his father wasn't well but could see nothing untoward. At sixty-five years of age he still cut a fit figure. He was solidly built but wasn't carrying any excess weight. He was almost as tall as Sam, although he'd shrunk a bit in the last ten years. His hair was now totally salt and pepper with no trace of the dark blond it had been. Even his beard was shades of grey. His hair probably needed a cut, a tidy-up, as did Sam's, but this was a legacy of not having a wife to remind him it was time for a visit to the barber. With his tanned, almost leathery skin, erect posture and greying hair he looked like a movie version of a sea captain. His eyes were brown; Sam had inherited his green eyes from his mother, but there was no debating the fact that his father, Sam and Sam's son, Edward, were three peas in a pod.

The noise of the engine prohibited conversation so the two of them followed their usual routines, just as they'd done for over twenty years. Sam rigged the rods, checked the bait, tossed a few cockles to the seagulls who always followed the boat for the first few kilometres and then did a few running repairs. Conversation could wait until they were fishing. They would have a few hours to discuss anything they needed to, which was more than enough time on any day. Today, in fact, Sam did want a sounding-board. He needed a sensible ear and his father, with his carefully measured manner, could usually be relied on to provide judicious advice.

'We might get lucky here,' his father said as he cut the engine. 'Snapper could be biting.' Together they baited hooks and cast the lines. Sam's father cleared his throat as they settled into their rhythm, a sure indication that today's fishing trip wasn't going to be the usual, mostly silent affair with a bit of general discussion. Throat clearing always preceded a father-son chat, as Sam thought of them, and had done so since he'd been a little boy. Something in Sam's behaviour must have suggested to his father that he needed a listening ear. Out on the water was the perfect time to embark on discussions. They were both comfortable at sea but having something to occupy themselves with, ensuring they didn't have to maintain eye contact, also helped.

'Juliet seems to be in good spirits,' Bob said. 'She tells me she's going to be fine. Is that right?'

'I hope so but it's really too early to know. She'll have to continue having blood tests and regular checks but the doctors are pretty confident that they've got everything. Jules took up every option that they offered her in terms of treatment.'

'And what are your plans for next year? You're going back to Sydney? Back to the navy?'

'I have to,' Sam replied. 'I've been trying to assess my options but if I want to stay in the navy then I can't see any other alternative.'

'What if Juliet needs more surgery or more chemo or radiotherapy? How are you going to manage the situation from Sydney?' Bob got a bite on his line and he jerked it back, hooking the fish and reeling it in as he continued. 'Even if there's nothing you need to do for Juliet, you need to think about the children. Someone has to look after them and even though you and Juliet are divorced they are still your children, still your responsibility.'

'I know that, Dad. I'm trying to do the right thing by everyone, but it's not easy. I wish there was a way I could have it all but I can't see that happening.'

'All?' Bob had his head down as he unhooked his catch before throwing it into a container filled with seawater, where it continued to swim around.

'Yes. I really don't want to give up the navy but I didn't want to give up my family either,' Sam said as he reeled in his line to check the bait. The bait was gone so he replenished it before casting out again, continuing the conversation as his hands stayed busy. 'I didn't want to get divorced but that's what I am, and I can't see how I can fix this.'

'You're not prepared to give up the defence force? Even now?' his father queried.

'The navy is all I know. It's what I'm good at.' Sam raked his fingers through his hair. 'I love my family, Juliet included, but I can't stand the idea of going to work for the next thirty years doing something I don't enjoy just to pay the bills. I need to be out at sea. I take after you there. Look at you, you're retired but you're still on the ocean almost every day.'

'Are you sure you're not using the ocean as an excuse?'

'An excuse for what?'

'Settling down, staying in one place. Are you avoiding family life? I would give all this up in an instant if it would bring your mother back. Once she died there didn't seem any reason not to stay with the navy. Your aunt Helen was happy to come with me and you were okay, but I would have preferred you to have had your mother.'

'I would have liked that too.'

'In a perfect world you would have had us both. Your kids can still have that.'

'But that's just it. I don't see how.' His father was watching him, he could feel it. Sam looked up from his line. 'What?'

'I'm just wondering what you'd do if, heaven forbid, Juliet doesn't make it. Would you drag your kids around the country then?'

Sam thought of Kate. She was coping well at the moment, and the time she was spending with both him and Juliet seemed to be easing her concerns. But if something else did go wrong he knew he wouldn't be able to move her without consequences. Juliet had been right about that. Kate needed constancy—she wasn't a child who coped well with change.

'No,' he replied.

'So why don't you look at what you'd do then? You don't have to wait for something else to go wrong if you can find a solution now.'

'But that's the problem. I can't think of any solutions.'

Juliet seemed to be doing so much better. Sam had thought about her not making it when she'd gone in for the mastectomy but since then he'd blocked from his mind the thought that it might not fix things. He didn't want to think about her not making it but maybe his dad was right. Maybe he could use that thought just as a hypo-thetical. He'd have to find a solution then.

'Can I make a suggestion?' Bob asked.

Sam nodded in response as he realised that this was what he'd been hoping for. He'd wanted another head to help solve his dilemma. 'Go for it.'

'There are jobs with the defence force that keep you in one place—'

'Desk jobs.' That was not what he wanted to hear. A desk job was not for him.

'They're probably desk jobs by definition,' his dad agreed, 'but they would allow you to be per-manently placed somewhere. If you considered teaching or operational positions, you might still have a little time at sea but you wouldn't have to be away for long stints or move every few years.'

'How do you know about these?' Sam asked as he wondered why he hadn't considered that angle.

'Because I thought about it when your mum died but with Aunt Helen's help, and you being the type of child you were, we managed the moves. Not all children are cut out for frequent changes. Not all children are like you. It's an option worth thinking about.'

Sam finally hooked a fish of his own and he thought about his dad's suggestion as he brought the fish in. Despite Juliet's cancer, the best days of his year had been the two months when he'd been surrounded by his family. He knew if it wasn't for Juliet's cancer he wouldn't have had those times, and while he wished for Juliet to get her health back, he was also glad that he'd had an opportunity to spend that time with his family.

Having them all together had reminded him of how much he loved them, of how much he needed them and how much they needed him.

He'd been trying to ignore how lonely he was going to feel after the end of this holiday.

He still believed, still hoped, that Juliet was going to be okay but a shore-based posting did have its merits. It would mean he could still be a part of the navy. The navy had made him the man he was, and he was reluctant to give it up if he didn't have to. Leaving the navy for a civilian life, even temporarily, had made him frustrated and angry and he didn't want to be that person again. He needed fulfilment in his career but this time he knew that if he had to sacrifice one or the other, this time his family would come first.

But what if he could find a shore-based position? It would mean he could be available if Juliet or the children needed him. And it could mean the difference between getting his family back or not. His dad was right—it was worth considering. It was his best option. It was his only option.

New Year's Eve, 2008

Juliet stepped out of the shower after rinsing the salt water from her skin. She wrapped herself in a towel and then squeezed the water from her bathers. She was slowly getting used to her naked appearance but she still preferred to avoid mirrors when she could. Once she was dressed it was a different story.

The surprise weekend shopping trip to Canberra that Sam had organised had been a chance to shop for bras, breast prostheses and swimming costumes. Juliet was happy with the results of her retail therapy session and although she hadn't been able to do much about her naked self yet, when dressed in a properly fitted bra and the right stuffing, she thought she looked okay.

The weekend in Canberra had been fabulous. Sam had been fabulous. The children had loved seeing the university oval where their parents had met, the Ferris wheel where Sam had proposed, the flat they'd first lived in. There had been a lot of good memories.

Juliet didn't know how she would have managed over the past couple of months without Sam's help and she'd agreed to spend this week in Merimbula with him as her way of saying thank you. She'd known he'd wanted her to join him and she'd had no reason to refuse.

They'd had five days in Merimbula already and the kids were having the time of their lives. How they were all going to cope when the time came to go back to Melbourne was concerning her a little, especially as they would be leaving Sam behind. His carer's leave would be finished and he was due to go back to Sydney.

But she had another two days before the trip was over and perhaps everything would be fine. She wasn't going to make a mountain out of a molehill and stress about things that might or might not happen. Reducing her stress levels had been part of the advice Dr Davey, the oncologist, had given her, and it was advice she was going to try hard to follow. Studies had shown that some cancers were stress related and she wasn't going to disadvantage her recovery by letting her imagination get the better of her and worrying about every little possibility.

She took a deep, calming breath, visualising all the pleasant things she and the children had been doing in Merimbula.

Bob's house was a gorgeous weatherboard cottage overlooking the sea about two kilometres from the centre of town. There weren't a lot of reasons in Juliet's mind to leave the cottage but they had ventured into town on pushbikes and pottered about down by the river that ran behind Bob's house. The children swam off the beach at Spencer Park, which was at the mouth of the river, while she rested in the shade. She had spent a fair bit of time eating the mangoes and strawberries that were in season and the freshly caught fish that Sam and Bob brought in most days. Sam had spent most of the time with them too, the only exception being when he went fishing with his father, but quite often he took one or both children too.

Juliet hadn't felt up to going fishing yet. She couldn't spend hours in the sun as the chemo had made her susceptible to sunburn and she didn't really have enough energy for fishing, but she'd been surprised to find how much she missed Sam's company when he was gone for a few hours. The time here was reminding her of the time they'd had in Bali all those years ago. She needed time to heal and with Sam's attention she could feel herself recovering.

She hung her towel on the rack and decided to

dress for a celebration—it was New Year's Eve after all.

She had packed carefully for the Christmas holidays, including most of her purchases from Canberra, telling herself that if she looked as good as possible it would boost her confidence. She knew that really she just wanted to look good for Sam. This week in Merimbula together was all about the children and ostensibly to give her a chance to rest and regain her strength, but it wouldn't hurt to look good.

She chose a white dress—her fair skin for once was lightly tanned and the dress would show off her tan and emphasise her arms. It had a modest neckline that allowed her to wear her new prostheses and she teamed it with a headscarf in a blue-and-white pattern that she knew brought out the colour in her eyes. If she was going to dress up, she might as well give it everything. Kate had bought her the scarf, with Sam's help, and had given it to Juliet for Christmas. Her hair had completely fallen out and she found her wigs were much too hot and uncomfortable to wear out in the sun to the beach or the river. Kate's scarf was perfect. She knew Kate had bought the scarf because she couldn't stand the thought of a bald mother, and Juliet was careful to keep her head covered when she was around the children.

She tied the ends of the scarf and let them fall loosely down her back before applying some mascara and lipgloss to make herself more presentable. Her eyelashes and eyebrows hadn't been affected by the chemotherapy drug, Cytoxan, probably because those hair follicles were slower growing than her head hair and she was grateful for some small mercies. Finally she was ready.

Sam had already taken the children down to the beach to get the bonfire started, and Sam's dad and aunt were celebrating New Year with friends so it was just the four of them having their own party on the sand. Juliet checked her reflection one final time and took another deep breath to calm her nerves as she remonstrated with herself about being foolish. She grabbed a warm coat, switched on a couple of lights and left the house to walk down the path to the beach.

Juliet had rested on the pillows Sam had carried down to the beach and watched him cook

fish and potatoes in coals taken from the bonfire while the children had toasted marshmal-
lows. For dessert Sam had split open bananas
and filled their centres with chocolate before
wrapping them in foil and baking them in the
coals. They'd eaten these while they'd watched
the nine o'clock fireworks display that lit up the
far end of the beach. It had been an almost perfect evening.

It was nearing midnight now but it was still a
glorious calm summer's night. There wasn't a
breath of wind but the temperature had dropped
slightly and the fire wasn't throwing any warmth
onto them now. It had burnt right down and all
that remained was a pile of glowing coals. The
kids had fallen asleep. Edward was tucked in
against Juliet's side and Kate was on her other
side, curled between her parents. Sam had set
up a groundsheet with cushions and quilts and
had covered them all with blankets. Juliet could
feel the cool air on her face but the rest of her
was surprisingly warm and comfortable. She
yawned.

'Have you had enough?' Sam asked, hearing
her yawn.

'No. I want to stay up for the midnight fireworks. I want to see in the New Year.' She looked down the beach. The local surf lifesavers had handed out glow-stick bracelets to revellers earlier in the evening and the beach was dotted with lights. At the far end, where the fireworks would be set off, a stage had been erected, a band was playing and the young adult crowd was partying in full swing.

'It's just another day. We should call it a night if you're tired.'

Juliet shook her head. 'It's more than another day. It's the start of a new year and it's a chance to move forward. I can't wait to put 2008 behind me—it wasn't the best year of my life.'

'I guess not.' Sam paused and flashed her his familiar, lopsided grin that instantly made her feel like the world was a better place. 'I'm really glad you're here, Jules. You had me frightened for a while—I wasn't sure that we were going to have another Christmas.'

'I told you I wasn't leaving my children.'

'I know. I'm just glad you meant it. How are you feeling, honestly? Are you ready for the year?'

'I feel good. I'm getting stronger every day. I just want things to go back to normal.' She still wasn't quite sure what normal was but it sounded like the right thing to say.

'Are you going to be okay?'

'I think so.'

She knew what he was really asking. She'd grown used to having Sam around. The children had too and Juliet knew they'd take some time to adjust back to being a family of three again. Making this transition again was what she'd been worried about when Sam had first moved back with them but the past couple of months had been worth it. She didn't think she would have managed without him. Once again, he'd been her rock.

'You were right, you know. I wouldn't have managed the past couple of months without you. Thank you.' It was important to her that he knew she was grateful.

'I'm happy I could help. You would have got through but if I've made things easier then I'm glad. That was my intention and I want you to know that you can call on me at any time, for anything, and I'll do my best to help. The children are still my responsibility and, despite everything, I still feel I have a responsibility to you too.'

She nodded and watched him as he lay on his back, propped on his elbows, one knee bent. He was simply gorgeous and her heart flipped in her chest. He still affected her as much as he had on the day they'd met. There remained a physical pull of attraction every time she saw Sam—her body still ached for his caress, she still craved his touch. He was her addiction and she was finding that being under the same roof as him, to have him so close yet untouchable, was becoming more and more unbearable. How she wished his priorities had been different. How she wished he could have put his family first.

She had set him free, hoping he would come back, and he was back, but only temporarily. He was there out of kindness and compassion, and when things had settled down again, he'd be gone.

She'd spent a lot of time over the past year wishing things had turned out differently, but she was still finding it difficult to reconcile her heart with the facts, although she was beginning to accept that some things couldn't be changed. But as she lay on the blankets with Sam just inches away from her she let herself imagine, just for a moment, that they were still a couple. She imagined reaching out to stroke his arm. She closed her eyes and she could imagine the feel of his body under her fingers, the soft hair on his forearm, the warmth of his skin. She could picture his fingers joining with hers, holding her hand, and she could imagine his touch; she could feel the shivers of pleasure that would shoot through her as their fingers locked together.

In her mind his fingers were now trailing up her arm, imprinting his mark onto her skin, brushing the nape of her neck as he pulled her towards him, his breath sweet on her cheek, his lips soft against hers. She could almost taste him, could almost feel the thrust of his tongue against hers, could almost hear his soft moan of pleasure.

Just the image of him holding her, loving her, was enough to warm her soul. There would never be anyone else for her, not while Sam still lived and breathed. She knew that. She would never love anyone else the way she loved Sam.

'What are you thinking about?' Sam's voice interrupted her reverie.

She opened her eyes, ridiculously disappointed to find that she wasn't wrapped in his arms, to find he was still on the other side of the blanket. She couldn't imagine him wanting her back in his arms but that didn't stop her from imagining how it would feel. 'Nothing really.' It was ridiculous to reminisce like this. Imagining things didn't change their reality. It didn't change the fact they were divorced. It didn't change the fact that in two more days she'd be returning to Melbourne without him.

But, just for tonight, she would let her imagination run wild. There would be plenty of time for reality when she returned to Melbourne.

He stood and stretched. 'It's nearly midnight,' he said.

He was silhouetted against the stars and Juliet's breath caught in her throat. 'Where are you going?'

'I have something for you.' He rummaged through a bag and withdrew a parcel. He knelt beside her on the blanket and passed her the package.

Juliet unwrapped the present. Inside was a silver link bracelet and hanging from the links were two small, thin, silver circles. She lifted the chain from its bed of velvet. Each disc was engraved, the first with the word *Kate*, the second with *Edward*. It was delicate and gorgeous.

'It's not to remind you of what's important,' Sam explained, 'you know that as well as I do. It's to remind you of what we created together. I'm hoping the new year will be a year in which you'll be able to celebrate being well and I'm hoping that this bracelet will serve as a reminder of all the people around you who love you.'

'It's perfect. Thank you.' It was beautiful and it was almost perfect, but it was missing a disc. Juliet couldn't help thinking that there should have been a third disc with Sam's name on it. But she didn't say that, she just undid the clasp and passed the bracelet to Sam, holding out her hand for him to fasten the bracelet around her wrist. His fingers were warm on her skin as he held her arm steady, his touch gentle yet strong, disturbing her senses, just as she'd imagined it would.

As he snapped the clasp shut the first midnight firework exploded in the sky above them.

He grinned at her, his familiar smile lighting up his face. 'Happy New Year, Jules.'

'Happy New Year,' she repeated. Her voice was quiet in contrast to the noise of the fireworks but Sam was so close there was no need to shout. He was kneeling mere inches from her side and as she watched he leant towards her, closing the distance between them until it was no more than a finger's space separating them. No more than a breath. His eyes were shining, the hazel flecks in the green almost undetectable as his pupils dilated. The light wasn't reaching his eyes, their faces were so close that the light couldn't penetrate. Their gazes were locked. Juliet could feel the tension sparking in the air around them. She sat, motionless, too afraid to move in case she broke the spell.

She closed her eyes, wanting, waiting for Sam's touch.

She licked her lips. She could feel the breath coming out of her, could feel it being expelled from her lungs in short, shallow bursts, felt it move over her moist lips. Her respiration was rapid, matching her pulse.

Sam's breath was warm on her face.

She waited for his kiss, certain it was inevitable.

His hand cupped the back of her head and his fingers brushed the nape of her neck.

She gasped as he tilted her face up to his and his lips brushed over hers, soft and tender.

She heard herself moan and then Sam crushed her to him, the tenderness swamped by far more primeval emotions. Hunger, desire and passion took over. She parted her lips, welcoming him back to her.

She was home. She was back where she belonged. There was no other way to describe it. The light that had been missing from her life was back. Sam was vital. She knew now she could exist without him but she wouldn't be living. A life without Sam was a half life.

Her heart and soul went into the kiss and she felt Sam respond. Time stood still. No, it was better than that. Time reversed. It was as though all the things that had gone wrong in her life had been imagined. She could feel Sam breathing life back into her soul, restoring her.

She embraced the feeling of rejuvenation. Embraced Sam. She let him fill her heart and mind, her body and soul, until she was overflowing. She held tight to him; she couldn't let him go.

He tasted like chocolate, his mouth soft and warm and sweet. She put a hand to his cheek. His stubble was rough under her fingers and his skin was hot to the touch. Sam pulled her down to the blanket, pinning her beneath him, his body hard and lean above her. She was vaguely aware of the fireworks continuing to explode in the sky; she could see the flashes of light through her closed eyelids and it felt as though the eruptions were keeping time with her heartbeat.

Sam deepened the kiss and Juliet forgot about the fireworks. Forgot about everything. For a moment it was just her and Sam, cocooned in a bubble, their own piece of time and space. She was shielded from the world, protected by Sam.

Gradually, though, the thin film of their bubble was penetrated by the outside world. The night grew silent and dark, the fireworks had finished. Voices carried to them, caught on the sea breeze, and Juliet remembered they weren't the only ones on the beach. The voices disturbed her, interrupted her and she pulled back, very slightly, as she became self-conscious.

'Time to go?' Sam asked.

Juliet wasn't sure. What was she going to? What would happen when they got back to the house? Would they continue where they'd left off? Should they continue? But one thing she did know was that they couldn't stay down on the beach all night. She nodded.

'I'll carry Kate up and come back for Ed.' In the heat of the moment Juliet had even forgotten about her own children, lying on the blankets beside her. Sam scooped up their sleeping daughter, carrying her easily back to the house before returning to douse the fire and collect Ed. Juliet carried the cushions and blankets and followed in Sam's footprints. She used his depressions to make the trek through the soft sand easier, even though his steps were far larger than hers and she had to stretch right out to match his stride.

Sam took Edward into his bedroom and Juliet waited on the veranda.

She couldn't go inside. She knew she'd feel hemmed in, contained, and she was worried that it would feel like the end of the evening. She wasn't ready for it to end just yet. She wasn't sure what she was ready for exactly so, for now, she leant on the veranda railing outside her room and took a deep breath, letting the night air fill her lungs.

Sam came back outside after carrying the children to their beds. Neither of them spoke. Sam stood beside her and his distinctive warm, spicy scent filled her nose, blocking out the smell of the sea. The beach in front of them was dark and the ocean stretched away to the horizon, blending with the sky. It felt as though they were floating in the night. They were surrounded by stars; millions of bright, glowing spots of light were strewn across the inky-black sky.

Juliet felt Sam reach for her and she turned, meeting him halfway. The light from the bedroom illuminated the left side of his face. Automatically she raised her hand, lifting her fingers to his face as she traced the lines in the corners of his eyes. She saw the right side of his mouth lift in a smile and her fingers moved to follow the movement of his lips.

Sam caught her fingers in his, taking them to his mouth and kissing the tips. Juliet closed her eyes as Sam took her thumb between his lips and slid it into his hot, moist mouth. A soft moan escaped from her as Sam sucked on her thumb. He lowered her hand and bent his head, covering her mouth with his, muffling her moans of pleasure. Juliet opened her lips, her tongue meeting his, joining with him, lost in the familiar and enchanting feeling of being in his arms again.

The evening air was cool and Juliet shivered as a light breeze blew across her back. Sam pulled away when he felt her tremble. He wrapped an arm around her shoulders and tucked her against his side, sharing his warmth. 'Let's get you inside.'

He took her hand and led her into her bedroom. The double bed was the dominant feature of the room but beside it was an old armchair. Sam skirted the bed as Juliet trailed behind him. He led her to the armchair and pulled her onto his lap.

Juliet didn't resist as Sam claimed her again, kissing her soundly. They had unfinished business and Juliet didn't stop to think where it might end. His hand was on her knee and she felt it slide under the hem of her dress, caressing the inside of her thigh and sending pulses of desire shooting up to the very centre of her soul. She could feel her body responding to his touch, feel herself getting moist; preparing to welcome him back.

Sam shifted Juliet's weight, moving her bottom farther into his lap, and she could feel his arousal pressing against her. Involuntarily she parted her legs slightly, ready for his touch, but his hand wasn't on her thigh now. She felt him reaching behind her, the fingers of one hand on the zip at the back of her dress. She looked down, watching as his other hand brushed over her breast. Except it wasn't her breast. It was only padding. She could see his hand touching the thin fabric of her dress but she could feel nothing. No desire. No spark. No fire. Nothing.

Nothing except a reminder of what had transpired. Of how she'd changed. Of what was missing. Of what had gone.

'Stop.' The word escaped from her lips before she had time to think about what she was doing. She stood up, almost leaping out of Sam's lap. She was aware of Sam's shocked expression. She watched his face, could see him trying to process what had happened. She took a step back, away from the chair, knowing he would reach for her.

'I can't do this.'

She turned and fled to the en suite bathroom. She shut the door, leaning against it before she turned the lock. She could hear Sam on the other side.

'Jules, what's wrong?' She felt the door handle jiggle behind her back and for a moment she panicked, thinking she hadn't locked it properly.

It held.

'Jules?'

She couldn't do this.

'Just give me a minute.' She stepped away from the door and leant on the basin, breathing deeply, trying to slow her racing heart. She glanced in the mirror. Her pale face stared back at her, her freckles dark against her skin, her eyes shiny with unshed tears.

'Come out and tell me what the matter is,' Sam pleaded. 'I can't help if I don't know what's wrong.'

'Wait. Please.'

'Open the door, Jules.' The door handle rattled again. 'You can't stay in there.'

Sam was right, she knew he was. She couldn't stay closeted in the bathroom. She was being ridiculous. But she couldn't go out there. Not yet.

She turned on the taps, splashing her face with cold water as she tried to gather her thoughts. She pulled a towel from the rack, burying her face in the soft folds. She knew he was right. They needed to talk; they probably should have talked before they'd started making out like a couple of horny teenagers.

She dried her face and opened the bathroom door. Sam was sitting on the bed but stood and crossed the room in two strides. He stretched out one hand to wipe the traces of a tear from her cheek. 'I'm sorry if I pressured you. I didn't mean to.'

'You didn't.' Juliet took a step forward and Sam wrapped her in his arms, holding her to him.

'I thought we wanted the same thing.'

She couldn't blame him for thinking that—she'd certainly been a willing participant. To a point. 'That wasn't the problem.' Her voice was muffled against his chest.

'I need to know what you're thinking, Jules. I need to know what you want.' He moved back a pace, creating some distance between them.

'I can't...' She broke off. How did she explain what she'd been thinking, what she'd been feeling?

'Can't what? Can't be with me?'

She nodded.

She saw Sam glance at the armchair but he obviously thought better of sitting there again. He tugged her towards the bed, sitting down beside her, not quite touching. He was frowning. 'Why not?'

She hesitated, uncertain about how to phrase her answer.

'Jules, you need to tell me what's going on. We need to clear the air. Perhaps we should have had this conversation before now but we are going to have it before we make any more decisions. I need to understand what's happening, how you feel. I'm not going to make assumptions again—that didn't turn out so well for us last time.'

He was right. It wasn't his fault and he deserved to know that. 'I'm scared,' she said.

He was still frowning and his green eyes were dark. 'Of making love?'

She shook her head. 'Of being naked,' she whispered. 'I don't look the same any more.'

'What difference does that make?'

'All I can think of is you'll look at me and see all the bits that are missing. I don't want you to be disappointed.'

'Disappointed? You think I'll be disappointed?' He gathered her hands in his. 'My darling girl, all I can think about is how lucky I am to have a second chance. I can't believe we're here, together. Disappointed is not how I'd describe myself. Let me tell you what I see when I look at you.' He held both her hands in one of his as he tilted her face up to look into her eyes. 'I see the most beautiful woman. The woman I adore. And when you were on my lap, all I was thinking about was how lucky I was. I wasn't thinking anything more than that.' He smiled, and the frown lines disappeared and his eyes lightened.

'Trust me, I'm not taking inventory. I don't care about the bits of you that are missing—all I care about is you. All I want is you.' He traced her lips with his finger before bending his head to kiss her cheek. 'But I can be patient.'

Wasn't he going to argue? Wasn't he going to try and convince her to spend the night with him? Disappointment flooded through her but before she could feel the pain of rejection she realised she was partly relieved too. She knew she wasn't ready. She knew that in her fragile state Sam could be more than she was ready to cope with. She wasn't confident enough to take things further. Not tonight.

Sam's fingers cupped her chin and his thumb brushed over her lips. Her lips felt swollen and tender under his touch. 'This is just the beginning, Jules. You need to know that.'

'The beginning of what?'

'The rest of our lives. I want a chance to make things right again. I've made a New Year's resolution—I want my family back and I'm prepared to make the changes necessary to achieve that. I've learnt a lot about myself in the past year and you were right—our family does need to come first. I love our kids and I love you. So, if you can give me a little time I'm going to do what I can to repair things and then maybe we can have a future. What do you think? Will you give me another chance?'

She wanted to say yes. Despite her cancer and the chemotherapy, the past two months had been better than she could have hoped for thanks to Sam's presence and assistance. Having him beside her had been what she'd dreamt of, what she'd wanted all along, but she still couldn't imagine how it could all work out now.

She wanted to say yes but she couldn't see how things could change. 'I don't see how we can work this out.'

'Just say you'll give me another chance and I'll worry about the rest.'

She nodded. She said yes. She knew she would always love Sam and having him in her life felt right, but she hoped she wasn't making another mistake.

* * *

They had two more days together before their holiday was over, before she took the children back to Melbourne and Sam left for Sydney. There were a few stolen moments—shared glances, a lingering touch of Sam's hand, a few passionate kisses—but there was no opportunity to take things further and Juliet was grateful for that as she was wavering in her thoughts and feelings. Not wavering exactly, more torn. When she was with Sam, all it took was one of his lopsided smiles and the touch of his fingers as he surreptitiously brushed her arm or thigh to make her feel like throwing caution to the wind. But when she caught a glimpse of herself in the mirror or thought about the reality of taking her clothes off, she didn't know if she could do it. She didn't know if she'd ever be able to. And where would that leave them? All Sam's planning would be pointless. She still couldn't see how this was going to work.

As their day of departure grew closer she knew she had some decisions to make.

She was worried now about returning to Melbourne without Sam. She was worried about how the children would cope. She had thought about this before, at the beginning, months ago, but somewhere along the way she'd become so caught up in the feeling of being part of a couple again that she'd ignored the fact that it was only a temporary arrangement.

Should she even be contemplating trying to repair her relationship with Sam?

Was she making a mistake?

If she was going to have a relationship with anybody, she needed some help. She would make an appointment with Ben McMahon, Gabby's brother, she decided. Plastic surgery might resolve her fears.

That was the easy decision.

That decision was made and then she would concentrate on the future. Would that future contain Sam? Could it?

CHAPTER NINE

IT TOOK them all some time to get used to being just the three of them again. Sam was back in Sydney, back to being a weekend father. Juliet was feeling good. The holiday and Sam's company had refreshed her but she was lonely. She knew she had to be careful. She missed Sam, she still had feelings for him, but even if he felt the same way, their circumstances hadn't changed and she couldn't afford to get carried away with the idea of salvaging their relationship.

She had to get on with her life.

She'd had an appointment with Ben McMahon to discuss reconstructive surgery and she had a date scheduled for the operation. She had promised Sam that he'd be the first person she'd call whenever she needed help with the children and, if he could, he would come down to Melbourne. It wasn't as good as having him in the same city but it was an offer that she would take him up on.

She dialled his number and after some preliminary chat brought up the reason for her call.

'I was wondering if you could do me a favour?' she asked.

'Sure.'

'I'm going into hospital for more surgery—'

'What's happened?' Sam interrupted. 'Is everything okay?'

'Everything's fine,' she said, trying to allay his fears. 'I've decided to have a breast reconstruction and I need to know if you can come down to Melbourne for a few days to look after the kids while I'm in hospital.'

'When?'

'I'm booked in for January the twenty-seventh.'

'That soon?'

Juliet wondered why it mattered how soon the operation was. In her opinion, the sooner the better. 'Ben has agreed to squeeze me in, then.'

'What time would you need me in Melbourne?'

'I get admitted at seven in the morning so I'd need you here the night before, on Australia Day.'

'Jules, I can't. We've got a huge day on the harbour for Australia Day celebrations. The entire Sydney fleet will be out on the water. I'd never be able to get down to Melbourne then. Do you have to go in that day?'

'That's when Ben has a spot. I want this done.'

'Why now? Are you sure you're ready for more surgery?'

It was her decision—why was he debating this with her? Losing her breasts had become a constant reminder of what she'd been through and since the bedroom disaster of New Year's Eve Juliet had known that she would have to have reconstructive surgery. In her mind she needed the surgery to help her believe she was winning the fight and she also knew that if she was ever going to be able to have a relationship again, with Sam or anyone else, she needed to feel, and look, like a woman again.

'I want this surgery. I want to look like me again. It's important.'

'You look good now, Jules, but if you're going to have the surgery, can't you wait a bit? I'm sure we can work out a date that suits us both.'

She didn't want to wait, she wanted the surgery done soon, she wanted to be put back together. She knew she needed it before she could move forward. And she'd wanted Sam's help but, as usual, there was a clash between his work commitments and his personal life and she knew work would triumph. She knew she was being unfair but she couldn't help it. She'd been spoilt by his attention before Christmas and it was difficult to come back down to reality with such a hard bump. Back to the days where work had been more important than family.

'Don't worry, I'm sure Mum or Maggie can help out,' she snapped at him. She could hear the bite in her tone but she couldn't help it. She should have known better and her foolishness made her angry.

'I'm sorry, Jules, but you know what the navy's like. Everything is planned so far in advance, I need a bit more notice.'

She did know what the navy was like. She knew very well. But that didn't make her feel any better. 'Sure. Forget I asked.'

She hung up the phone, feeling ridiculously annoyed and frustrated and angry. Sam had *asked* her to call if she needed help and stupidly she'd taken him at his word. She'd actually thought she might be able to rely on him, but all his platitudes about how important his family was had been just talk. Nothing had changed. Sam had learnt nothing from the weeks they'd spent together as a family last year. Already work was his number-one priority. Maybe he saw elective surgery as not important but she wasn't going under the knife without due consideration. It was about more than just her physical appearance. She needed this emotionally as well.

Her feelings for Sam had been a big influence on her decision to have this surgery and now she felt like a fool. Why had she thought this would make any difference? She should have known better.

27 January 2009

Once again it was Maggie who came to help and, even though she was all Juliet needed, when it came time to be admitted to hospital Juliet was still irritated that Sam hadn't made it.

She tried not to be disappointed, tried not to worry, but the feeling that he should be there was almost too strong for her to ignore. But there wasn't anything she could do about it. She had to get on with things, had to move ahead.

'Morning, Juliet, how are you feeling?' Ben McMahon stepped into her room. She'd been impressed with his knowledge and confidence and his natural, easy bedside manner at her first appointment and hadn't hesitated to choose him as her surgeon. 'I just thought I'd go over the basics with you once more, to make sure you've got everything straight in your mind.' He'd had a clear vision and understanding of what she needed and she was comfortable with her decision but still nervous about the actual operation. She knew that Ben had realised this and was there to try to set her mind at ease.

She greeted him and watched as he took the few steps he needed to cross the room. He was wearing a navy suit with a blue shirt that matched his eyes and he was smiling. He had a nice smile that framed a set of even, white teeth and he was tall, dark and handsome, if you went for that type. Personally she preferred her men tall, blond and handsome, with green eyes and a lopsided smile.

'Now, remember, this is just the first step. I'm going to implant the tissue expander under your chest muscle and the second step will start in a fortnight when we begin the weekly procedures to inject the saline solution into the expander. Depending on how easily your skin stretches, it may take between six and eight weeks before there's enough space to swap the expanders for the implants. You'll have little or no feeling in your breasts as this is purely cosmetic, and if you decide you want a nipple reconstruction I'll have to do that at a later stage. Is that how you understood the plan?' Juliet nodded. 'Do you have any questions?'

'I don't think so.'

'All right. The anaesthetist will be in to see you shortly. We've discussed your reaction last time and he's going to give you something for the nausea while you're under anaesthetic. I'll see you in Theatre.'

The anaesthetist came and the nurse came, but the constant checks just added to Juliet's feeling of disquiet. Her nerves were building and, to make matters worse, as she was being wheeled off for surgery she recalled the dream she'd had following the mastectomy—when she'd watched the faceless woman walk off with her family. Her replacement.

Her nervousness intensified but overriding it all was her irritation with Sam. His offers of help had been empty promises, his words worthless. At least she knew there was no point in trying to salvage their relationship. She had to move on, for her own sake. She needed to be independent. Thank goodness she hadn't done anything foolish while they'd been in Merimbula. The reality was she was still on her own and Sam, despite his promises, had still put work first. Nothing had changed and she was glad they hadn't taken things further.

Somehow now she even felt like blaming him for the dream she'd had. As if he'd put the idea into her head. She knew she was supposed to remain as calm as possible, she knew that the more stressed patients were before surgery the worse their recovery was, and she knew that was why Ben had stopped by earlier—he'd been trying to set her mind at ease. But nothing had worked. She was cross and concerned now and there was no time to calm herself down. She could almost feel her blood pressure rising and there was nothing she could do about it.

The light was incredible, as though the whole sky was glowing. Juliet looked up and was surprised to find it wasn't the sky but the air itself that shone. Almost as though each little oxygen particle had its own light source within it. The light was bright and reminded her of those hot summer days when, as teenagers, she and her sister had lain at the beach, sunbathing, and they'd had to close their eyes against the glare of the sun. But even with your eyes closed the sun still shone through your eyelids, as though your eyelids were made of gauze.

But this light didn't hurt her eyes—she didn't need to close them. This light was welcoming. This light was like a living thing.

She stretched out one hand, thinking she'd be able to touch it, but of course there was nothing there.

It was warm, though. Juliet hadn't realised how cold she was but she could feel the light landing on her skin, wrapping around her, enveloping her, warming her, and she knew she was safe.

She walked into the light, wanting to feel its warmth on her skin. She turned round, letting the light warm her back.

Now she could smell fresh grass. Where was she? She had no recollection of being anywhere. She looked down, expecting to see grass under her feet, but there was nothing, just the light.

No, there was something beyond the light. People. They were busy, moving quickly. Coming and going around a central point like bees buzzing around a hive. What were they doing?

She frowned and looked up again, turning round in a slow circle. The light was all around her now but there was nothing else. No landmarks, no people, no sky, no ground. Nothing.

'Juliet. Juliet, can you hear me?'

The voice was coming from her left. She turned but there was still nothing to see. Nothing but the light.

'Juliet.'

She thought she recognised the voice now—it was her brother-in-law.

'Steven?'

She took a step towards him.

'No!'

She stopped and her brother-in-law spoke again. 'You can't do this, Juliet. Can you hear me?'

'Yes.'

'It's not your time yet.'

She frowned. He wasn't making any sense—her time for what? 'What are you talking about?'

'Juliet, not now. Your children need you.'

And then she remembered. Steven was dead, he'd been dead for ten years.

The shock went through her like a bolt of lightning.

The light, Steven's voice, this was what people talked about.

She looked down again. That was her in the middle of the circle of people. She was the bee-hive. All those busy people were buzzing around her. But while they were busy, she was still, lying on a table, immobile. She kept watching and saw one person lean forward as the others took a step back.

'This time, Juliet.'

She looked back towards Steven's voice as a second bolt of lightning hit her. She couldn't speak, couldn't breathe, and then the light faded to black.

He was gone and she was alone again.

'Juliet, can you hear me?'

No, she wasn't alone; he was still there. 'Steven?' She tried to open her eyes but her eyelids were too heavy.

'It's Ben, Juliet. You're in hospital. You're in the operating theatre. Everything's all right now.'

Ben? She didn't know anyone called Ben.

She was tired and cold. She just wanted to be warm.

27 January 2009

Sam was exhausted. The Australia Day celebrations had been a huge exercise—just the final details alone had taken up almost every minute of the three weeks he'd been back at work. But now it was over. He'd debated jumping on the first flight to Melbourne that morning to be at the hospital for Juliet but she'd quickly put an end to that, telling him Maggie would be there and she would let him know how the surgery went. He knew she was mad with him, he knew she'd expected him to be there for her. He couldn't blame her really. He had asked her to call him for help and the first time she'd done it he'd been tied up with work. Again.

But surely she could have delayed the surgery? It was only cosmetic after all.

Everything they'd achieved before Christmas had unravelled in the space of one conversation. They were back to square one, divorced and living in different cities.

He'd spoken to his captain about a desk job but he wasn't even sure if that would be enough.

The morning dragged as he waited for Maggie's call but when it came it wasn't the news he'd been hoping for.

He snatched his phone up as it buzzed on his desk.

'Maggie?'

'Hi, Sam.'

'How is she?'

'Um, there have been some complications.'

'What's happened? Is she okay?'

'She's okay now but apparently she had a reaction to one of the drugs.' Maggie paused. 'They had to resuscitate her.'

'Resuscitate her!' Oh, God. Sam was grateful he was already sitting down. He put his head between his knees. He thought he was going to throw up.

'Sam? Are you still there? Are you okay?'

He was perfectly okay. It was Juliet who wasn't. His father's words were repeating themselves in his head. *I'm just wondering what you'd do if, heaven forbid, Juliet doesn't make it. Would you drag your kids around the country then?*

He hadn't thought his father's words would be so accurate. But it sounded like he'd come within a whisker of being in exactly that situation. What would he do?

'What happened? Do you know?'

'Her blood pressure was quite high when she went into Theatre and they gave her something to bring it down. They gave her some anti-nausea medication as well to try to eliminate the nausea she experienced last time and they think she had a reaction to that, which further dropped her blood pressure. She's out of danger now and the doctor says she'll be fine. We have to believe him, we have no other choice.'

'Can I speak to her?'

'Not yet.'

'What about the doctor, Ben? Can I speak to him?'

'I'll ask the nurses to get him to ring you and I'll let you know if anything changes. I'll take care of her, Sam.'

He knew she would but he wanted to do it. Juliet was his girl. Even though they were divorced he still thought of her as his and he knew he always would. He had tried to do the right thing for his family by letting them stay in Melbourne but he should have stayed there too. He realised that now. Now more than ever.

He'd done it again. He'd let work dictate his life. He'd learnt nothing.

No. That wasn't true. He'd learnt but he'd been too slow.

He wasn't going to sit in Sydney any longer.

He was on the next plane to Melbourne.

He was going to get his wife back.

He hadn't counted on not being allowed to see her.

'I'm sorry, visitors are strictly limited in Intensive Care,' the nurse told him.

'But I'm her husband.' Sam struggled to keep his voice down as he stretched the truth just a little. He hadn't come there only to be foiled at the last hurdle.

The nurse was flicking through Juliet's chart. 'You're not listed as her next of kin. You'll have to wait for the doctor. If he thinks she's up to an extra visitor then maybe you can see her.'

'Can you ring Dr McMahon for me? He's a friend of the family.' Sam stretched the truth a little more in the hope the nurse would be persuaded to do him a favour. He needed to see Juliet now.

'He should be here shortly,' the nurse said, her tone terse. 'If you have his number, you can call him.'

Sam's ploy had backfired. He didn't have Ben's number, he'd only met him once, so he had no choice but to sit and wait. 'If you're expecting him soon, I'll wait. No need to bother him unnecessarily,' he replied, not wanting the nurse to think she'd had the last word.

'Sam! Are you waiting to speak to me?'

Sam stood as Ben arrived and shook his hand. 'I'm actually waiting to see Juliet.'

'What's the hold-up?'

Sam inclined his head towards the nurses' station. 'I'm not listed in her chart—that makes me *persona non grata*. I need your permission.'

'She's doing fine. Just let me do a quick check and then she's all yours.' Ben disappeared into the intensive care unit with the battleaxe of a nurse trailing behind. Sam watched from the doorway, looking for Juliet's bed.

'She's pretty drowsy but you can have a few minutes with her,' Ben said as he came out.

Sam didn't need to be told twice.

She was so still. So tiny. Her head was bare, no wig, no scarf to cover her scalp, and Sam was momentarily surprised. He hadn't seen her without some sort of head cover and although her hair had started to grow back, regrowth was minimal and the soft cap of downy hair was barely noticeable. If he hadn't seen which bed Ben had gone to Sam doubted he would have recognised her. He double-checked the name tag above the bed.

He dragged a chair closer to the bed.

'Jules?'

Her hand was resting on top of the sheet.

He covered her hand with his and she opened her eyes.

'Hi.' He squeezed her fingers.

She smiled and a tidal wave of relief rushed over him. His eyes were burning and he could feel tears gathering.

'You're okay.' He leant forward and carefully kissed her cheek, mindful of the tubes and wires connecting her to the various pieces of equipment.

He sat in the chair. 'I'm so sorry I wasn't here earlier. If I'd known...' How could anyone have predicted this? And what would he have done? His words tapered off. Juliet had closed her eyes and she said nothing. What could she say? The silence was broken only by the rhythmical *blip-blip* of the monitors.

Sam watched her, making sure she was breathing, watching the numbers on the monitor, waiting for her to speak. But there was nothing. Was she sleeping?

'I've let you down again, haven't I?' He spoke to the silence. 'I'm going to make up for it. I promise.'

Juliet's monitors started beeping. The *blip-*

blip changed to a buzzing sound. What did that mean? Was it an alarm? Sam looked up at the screen but, of course, the lines and numbers meant nothing to him. But none of the numbers read zero so he supposed that was a good thing.

The nurse bustled in; she pressed a button that switched off the alarm as she checked the screen.

'You'll have to leave now,' she told Sam.

'Is everything all right?'

'She needs peace and quiet. She doesn't need any more excitement. She needs to rest.'

Sam didn't know where the nurse had got the idea that he was exciting Juliet. She seemed quite calm to him, but he knew the nurse was taking great delight in being able to evict him from the ICU. He wouldn't argue. As long as Juliet was okay, he wasn't going to make a scene.

He stood up and kissed Juliet again, aware of the nurse watching him closely. 'I'll be back and I'll do a better job next time, I promise,' he whispered to Juliet before he left the unit. Having seen her with his own eyes, he felt much better. The visit had reassured him and he knew the trip had been worthwhile. He could go now and if he got a chance he would come back again before he had to return to Sydney. The nurse had asked him to leave but she hadn't said he couldn't come back.

Sam had promised Juliet he'd fix things. He'd promised twice. But while he had put the wheels in motion he now needed to speed things up—he couldn't afford not to. He needed to speak to his captain again.

There were signs everywhere reminding visitors not to use mobile phones so Sam left the hospital building before dialling his superior's number.

'Sir, it's Sam Taylor.'

'Sam. What can I do for you?'

'I'm just following up on our conversation regarding permanent postings. I need to know about the next available position in Melbourne— whatever it is.' He had broached the subject when he'd returned from leave and had known it could take a while before something suitable came up, but that hadn't bothered him at the time. Now he wanted something, anything, as soon as possible.

'Why the rush?'

'Juliet's not well,' he said, then explained what had transpired in surgery. 'I need to be there. I need to be there soon.'

'I'll see what I can do.'

'Thank you, sir.' Sam knew his captain didn't want to set him up with a permanent posting. He didn't want to lose him and he'd told him that much in their first meeting, but Sam trusted him to keep his word and he knew the other man would do his best to find something. He just hoped it wouldn't take too long.

CHAPTER TEN

February 2009

SOMETIMES Juliet wondered if she'd dreamt Sam's visit to Melbourne when she'd been in the ICU. Her recollection was vague at best but Ben had confirmed that she hadn't imagined it. Sam hadn't stayed for long but he'd promised to return and now he was coming to Melbourne for the weekend. He was still promising to fix things but Juliet wasn't putting much stock into that. He was being very cagey about his plans, and had told Juliet he was sorting some stuff out and would explain when he got there. He was coming to watch Kate in a ballet recital but Juliet didn't know anything more than that.

All the progress Kate had made prior to Christmas had unravelled since Juliet's 'incident', as she thought of it. Kate had barely left her side and had refused to go to school on several occasions. Juliet had been forced to sit through numerous ballet rehearsals just to ensure that Kate would stay and it had been exhausting. Juliet understood that Kate was afraid but nothing she said seemed to ease her daughter's fears. Juliet was at a loss as to what else she could do.

Fortunately Maggie was still in Melbourne and she'd borne the brunt of taking care of Edward's extra-curricular activities, but Juliet was hoping that Sam's presence would divert Kate's attention and give her some time to spend with Ed. She was looking forward to a break from Kate's constant shadowing and the thought made her feel like a bad mother, but she was finding it rather trying. She hoped the double excitement of the recital and Sam's visit would help to keep Kate's mind occupied. Perhaps, when the weekend was over, Kate would have forgotten her fears and her need to keep Juliet close. Or perhaps that was wishful thinking.

The recital went well. Kate was in high spirits and her excitement increased when Sam announced he was taking them all to Sofia's for dinner. Juliet wanted to refuse Sam's invitation because she was still annoyed with him, but she agreed to go to dinner because she didn't want to disappoint the children. She didn't want to be like Sam and put more importance on her own feelings than on those of her children. It was bad enough that one parent had higher priorities than the family. She wasn't going to go down that same path.

Juliet was still giving off a frosty vibe. There was no doubting that she was still mad with him but at least she'd agreed to join them for dinner. He had something important to tell them all and on neutral ground was a good place to do that.

Sam waited until dessert was served before he began. The children were focussed on their usual order, a massive serving of *gelati* each, four scoops of different flavours, which would be enough to keep them occupied for the next twenty minutes, or until it melted over the table, which would give Sam enough time to make his announcement.

'I have some news.'

'Good news?' Juliet asked. She looked wary.

'I hope so. I've got a temporary posting to HMAS *Cerberus*.'

'What's that?' Edward asked.

'It's the navy base down south, sort of on the way to Philip Island. It's where I'm going to be working for a while,' he explained.

'It's near us?' Ed clarified.

Sam nodded. 'It's in Victoria.'

'We can see you every day?'

'It's about an hour and a half away so I'm going to stay down there during the week, but I can see you every weekend and I'll be able to come up to Melbourne whenever you need me.'

Juliet was staring at him. She'd said nothing. Something was bugging her.

'What is it?' he asked.

'Can we talk about this later?' She glanced at the children. They'd forgotten about their *gelati* and were concentrating on the conversation. Sam recognised Juliet's body language. They were obviously heading for a discussion that needed to be out of earshot of the children.

He'd hoped it would be good news; he'd thought he was making a good decision, but he must have got it wrong. Again.

'Sure.' He picked up a spoon and pinched a taste of Ed's dessert, changing the topic completely to avoid an argument in public. 'Looks like you're gonna need help with that one, mate,' he said as he swallowed a mouthful of chocolate *gelati* and tried to ignore Juliet's icy expression. He just hoped she would calm down before they got home.

But he was out of luck. He drove them all back to the house, his old home, and the conversation continued once the children were in bed.

'What's the problem with this posting?' he asked. 'I thought you'd be happy to have me close by. I thought it would take some pressure off you.'

'It's a temporary posting, you said?' Her voice was tight and her blue eyes flashed fire. He recognised that look—she was ready for an argument.

He nodded and decided to stick to answering her questions as straightforwardly as possible. There was no point in fanning the flames of her anger by telling her things she didn't want to hear. So, until he worked out what she wanted, he thought it best to keep things simple. He thought he was less likely to get into trouble that way. 'Until July, at this stage.'

'And why are you taking it?'

'So I can spend time with the kids. So I can give you a hand.'

'For five months and then what? We're back to the same point again. You'll move on. We'll stay here.'

It wasn't a question.

'You're welcome to move with me.' His mouth was faster than his brain. He hadn't meant to say that, even though it was true. She glared at him, and he tried again. 'I thought a few months would be a good start. I thought it would be better than nothing and maybe it will lead to something more permanent.'

'But it might not.'

'It might not,' he agreed.

'And that's my point. I understand you're doing this for the right reasons, and you think you're helping, but all you're doing is delaying the inevitable. You won't be here for ever.'

He would be filling in for another officer who had been diagnosed with cancer. It was unlikely that officer would return to the job, in which case, if Sam was happy, the position could become his permanently, but he didn't want to make assumptions at this stage and he didn't want to bring up the subject of a colleague with terminal cancer. He'd be best sticking to a simple explanation. 'It was the best I could do at short notice.'

His response didn't seem to appease Juliet.

'If you can do this now, why couldn't you do it eighteen months ago?'

Because he hadn't thought about it. Probably best not to say that. 'These jobs don't come up often. People tend to hang on to them,' he replied.

'But why now?'

'The kids need me.' This was part of the answer but not the whole truth.

'They needed you eighteen months ago too.'

'I know and I'm sorry that it's taken me this time to realise that. I admit, if it hadn't been for your health I probably still wouldn't see it your way. But you were right when you wanted to keep the family together. I didn't realise, I didn't see why it was so important. My childhood was very different from most but I didn't know anything else and I couldn't see why having two parents was so important. One good full-time parent was more than most kids had and ours had you plus me when I was home. I figured as long as the children had you, that would be fine. But...'

He was hesitating with his explanations now, finding it difficult to explain his feelings and reasons. He hadn't really thought this part through and he was heading into territory that was a bit risky. Territory that could open up arguments.

'But what?'

'But you gave me a hell of a fright with your drama in hospital and I thought what if—?'

'What if they don't have me?' Juliet finished his sentence. As usual she knew what he was thinking.

'Yes. But it's not as sudden as it seems. Spending those months with you prior to Christmas made me realise how much I'd missed you, missed you all, and I didn't want to go back to Sydney. I wanted to be with my family. Or at least nearby. When I got back I put some feelers out, trying to work out how I could arrange things, but your experience in hospital made me realise that perhaps I didn't have the luxury of time. I had to have something quickly.'

'And this is it? This is the job you want?'

'I don't know.' He felt it was important to be honest, even if it meant heated discussion ensued. He couldn't afford there to be any misunderstanding. 'But, even if it's not, my priorities have changed. My job doesn't come first any more. I know you think I gave up too easily last time. I know you think I should have put my family first, and I agree with you now. I made a mistake. Nearly losing you has put things into perspective. I'm trying to fix things. Taking this position is the first step. I want a chance to prove to you that things are different. That I've changed.'

'But don't you see? Nothing is different, nothing has changed,' Juliet argued. 'You made me promise to call you first if I needed help, if the children needed you, but where were you when I went into hospital in January? You still had work commitments. Nothing changed.'

He wanted to tell her that wasn't fair. She hadn't given him fair warning. 'I thought I had time.' Time to fix things. But he'd been forced to act quickly and he just hoped he could get it right.

But Juliet hadn't finished with him. 'This latest surgery was just step one of the reconstruction. Where will you be six weeks' time when I go into hospital again? You're not only telling me you'll be around to help but you're promising the children you'll be around for them too. How is that possible? You're still an officer in the navy. You're still going to be doing the navy's bidding, put their demands first. That's what you have to do as long as you are serving with the defence force. I get that but I don't think you do.'

'This job is different—this is a shore-based position.'

'Shore based! Why are you interested in it if you're stuck on land? I thought that was a deal-breaker before.'

She was right. He'd hated the job with the oil company but it wasn't solely because it had been land based. 'There were lots of things wrong with the civilian job. For a start this one is still with the defence force, so I keep my rank and all my entitlements.' He tried to explain. 'The navy is the only life I've ever known. I grew up as a defence force kid, I was surrounded by defence force personnel and their families all my life and that's how I see myself. When I took the civilian job I lost my identity. I like the structure and formality of the defence force. I define myself by the code of the navy and when I took leave I lost something of myself in the process. That was the biggest problem, but I didn't realise it at the time. Leaving the navy diminished me in my own eyes, to the point where I lost respect for myself and I had nothing to give you. I need the navy but I also need you. My life doesn't work when I only have one. I can't be the man you need without the navy and this might be the perfect solution for us. For our family.'

'How do you figure that?'

'I'm going to be running training courses within the engineering faculty for electronics, technical and marine, with a bit of ship safety and survival training work as well. I'll be on base Monday to Friday, no weekends.'

'Monday to Friday? So you *will* be around for the children?'

'There will be a few trips to sea—' He broke off when Juliet gave him 'the look'. He clarified his statement. 'There are some overnight trips out into the bay for training purposes—firefighting and technical pracs, that's all.' Selling this posting was proving much harder than he'd expected. He'd really thought it would be an easy exercise, an opportunity too good to pass up and one that would suit everybody. 'I thought this would be a win-win situation for us all.'

'So you're doing this for us?'

He nodded. 'I want my family back, Jules. You included.'

'You want us back? What does that mean exactly?'

'I love you, Jules. I always have and I always will. It's not too late for us. I know it's not. We can have a second chance. You just have to give it to me.' He knelt on one knee and took one of her hands in his, holding tight just in case she wanted to pull away. 'I want my family back, Jules. I love you and I want you to marry me.'

'Don't be ridiculous. Get up.' She snatched her hand back. She definitely wasn't seeing his vision. 'This changes nothing. It's a temporary posting, you said so yourself. I appreciate what you're doing but please don't assume that it's going to change things between us. I can't rely on you and I'm not going to pretend that I will. I know I have to get on with things on my own. I think you're making promises you can't keep and I need to do what's right for the children, and that includes putting my needs first too. I have to move on. It's over, Sam.'

He supposed he deserved that. He might be in for a long battle but it was one he was determined to win. He enjoyed a challenge and he didn't doubt Juliet would test his resolve, but he had no intention of going down without a fight this time. There was too much at stake. 'I'm going to keep proposing until you say yes,' he declared.

'Well, I hope you don't mind disappointment.'

Sam wasn't too disheartened. He knew Juliet—he knew exactly how stubborn she could be, and he'd never expected it would be easy to convince her to give him another chance. But he knew that if he could plant an idea, and give her time to get used to it, maybe she'd even eventually think it had been her suggestion. If he could show her he was serious, show her he was committed to his family and to her, then perhaps she'd start to see his point of view and perhaps he'd get what he wanted. Perhaps he'd get her back.

CHAPTER ELEVEN

June 2009

JULIET lay in bed, a year's worth of thoughts running through her head. Today was her birthday and it was almost impossible to believe what had transpired over the previous twelve months. From one birthday to the next she had gone from being a healthy, married mother of two to a divorced mother of two recovering from breast cancer. Not a great year. But, she thought, at least she'd made it this far.

Her overwhelming feeling was one of relief. Her last blood-test results had been good and she'd actually made it through the final stage of the breast reconstruction without any dramas. She'd had the tissue expanders replaced with the implants and that had marked another step in her recovery process, a step in the right direction. Physically she was complete. The breast prostheses had been relegated to the back of a drawer. They'd served a purpose but she was glad to see the last of them, and her wigs were in boxes on top of the wardrobe. They would eventually end up in the dress-up box. Her hair was a few inches long now, long enough to be styled into an authentic pixie cut, similar to the wig she'd worn, but she'd stuck to her own hair colour. She was a brunette again. Her hair colour she was used to, her new breasts were taking a little longer to feel as though they belonged.

She was lying on her back and she looked down at her chest. She was still getting used to seeing her boobs pointing at the ceiling when she was lying down instead of disappearing under her armpits. That thought made her smile. Ben had used teardrop-shaped implants because they looked more natural than round but, still, when she was lying down they were obviously fake because they were unaffected by gravity. And they felt heavy. But it was nice not having to worry about stuffing her bra with prosthetic breasts or worrying that the prostheses had slipped out of position or looked lopsided.

Yes, a lot had changed in the past year but

overall things were looking up. She'd made it this far. Was there any harm now in planning for the future? What did she want it to bring her?

She knew what today was bringing her. It was bringing Sam.

They were going to celebrate her birthday as a family. He was still trying to convince her to make it official. He was still proposing every chance he got and she was still refusing. She wondered how long he would persist. She loved him, there was no doubting that, but in her mind they were going around in circles. Loving each other wasn't enough.

The last four months had unfolded just as Sam had told her they would. He'd been living on the naval base, ninety minutes from Melbourne, but he'd kept his part of the bargain and had spent weekends in town, just as he'd promised the children, and they loved having him around. Juliet enjoyed his company too—she didn't pretend otherwise, and she was more than happy to celebrate her birthday with Sam, but she wasn't planning any further than that.

The children were incredibly excited about the day's outing and that made everything worthwhile. Ed was at the age where he needed his dad. He needed the physical rough and tumble that he got from Sam, and Juliet wasn't up to that at the moment so Sam's presence was especially important. Kate's anxieties had diminished as well with the increased amount of time she was able to spend with both her parents. Juliet had to admit there were plenty of positives for their family with Sam's transfer to Victoria but it was still temporary. The kids were happy but she was hesitant about enjoying his company too much because, in the back of her mind, there was always the thought that he'd be gone again.

But there was no denying they still had a connection, one that had nothing to do with their children and everything to do with chemistry. All it took was a glance, an unconscious touch of his hand or one of his lopsided smiles and Juliet could feel herself falling under his spell. She had managed to refuse all his proposals so far but a girl could only resist so many times and she was fighting it with everything she had.

She got out of bed. It was time to get up. Time to get on with the next year of her life.

When she opened the door to Sam an hour

later she was surprised to see him standing there empty-handed. She'd assumed he'd give her yellow tulips, just as he'd done every birthday since they'd got engaged. Yellow tulips were their thing. He'd never forgotten before, which could only mean that it was a deliberate omission today.

She swallowed her disappointment. Every day she had was a bonus and she wasn't going to waste time sulking. Sam certainly had no obligation to buy her anything any more and she shouldn't expect him to. She was determined to enjoy the day.

'Happy birthday.' He greeted her with a smile, his unique, irresistible smile, and her petulance vanished in an instant. She forgot all about the tulips as she let the warmth of Sam's smile wash over her. He bent forward, kissing her cheek, and she closed her eyes and savoured the soft touch of his lips on her skin.

There wasn't time for a prolonged greeting as Kate and Edward arrived at the door in a flurry of excitement. They were heading for the Dandenong Ranges, south-east of Melbourne, where they were going for a ride on Puffing

Billy, a restored steam train, and Edward had been bouncing off the walls since early morning, bubbling with anticipation. Juliet had read the entire collection of 'Thomas the Tank Engine' stories to Ed when he'd been younger and this excursion was still one of his favourite things to do. They all loved this trip through the hills, which was why she'd chosen it as her outing.

There were some intermittent showers as they wound their way in the car through the foot-hills but by the time they reached Belgrave the rain had eased, although low mist still hugged the treetops and obscured the sun. The air smelt clean and fresh with an underlying scent of eucalyptus, and drops of moisture fell from the grey leaves of the gums and wet their heads as they walked beneath the trees and made their way to the station.

The train was waiting at the platform, steam billowing from its chimney as it waited for its next departure. Edward dragged Sam to the front of the train, watching in fascination as the engineer stoked the fire.

'We'll buy tickets and get some seats,' Juliet called to Sam as she and Kate headed for the ticket window. They found seats looking out over the platform and waited for the boys to join them. The carriages had bench seats and the top half of the carriage sides was open with just a couple of horizontal bars dividing the space. Green tarpaulins made makeshift walls but these were rolled up out of the way for the journey to allow the passengers to enjoy the view. The children scrambled to the sides of the carriages and clambered up to sit on the edge, legs dangling outside the carriage, bodies inside and arms clinging to the horizontal bars.

Despite the fact that her children, and hundreds of others, assumed this position every trip, Juliet was always nervous. She had one hand ready to reach for Ed if he started to topple and she jumped as the sound of the train's whistle pierced the stillness of the morning. A cloud of steam drifted past their window as the train lurched and began to pull away from the platform, and the children cheered as the train gathered speed.

'Relax! He'll be fine—he always is,' Sam said.

He was sitting opposite her and he recognised her discomfort, knew she was always worried about the perceived danger. He reached across and rubbed her knee, shooting a smile in her direction. A delicious tingle raced through her with his touch and she felt her nervousness abate. She took a deep breath and relaxed into her seat, reminding herself that she was going to have fun and commit every minute of the day to memory. The scent of eucalyptus was strong in the air, released from the leaves of the trees by the recent rainfall, and the rocking of the train was hypnotic. She closed her eyes briefly as the fresh air rushed over her face, ruffling her short hair. The noise of the train's wheels clacking on the rails made conversation almost impossible so Juliet didn't bother attempting to make small talk and instead watched as the world went past.

The train pulled into Emerald station, where they were stopping for lunch before returning to Belgrave. The sun had come out and the air was muggy with humidity. The kids stripped off their jackets and handed them to Juliet before racing off. There was a model railway exhibit here, which was Ed's second favourite thing after the train ride. Sam had given them money for the entrance fee and they wanted to make the most of the time they had before they'd be called back for a picnic lunch. Sam carried the basket he'd packed and they walked together looking for a spot to settle.

'Sun or shade?' Picnic tables were being claimed quickly but Sam had a picnic rug under his arm so they were self-sufficient.

'I'd like a bit of time in the sun—it's such a beautiful day now,' Juliet said as she pointed to her left. 'Under that tree looks like a good spot.'

She shrugged out of her coat as Sam spread the blanket on the ground. He opened the basket and started to pull out provisions.

'I can do that if you want to catch up to the kids,' Juliet offered. She unpacked hard-boiled eggs, ham and salad sandwiches and lemon tarts. Sam brought cold drinks back with him and they shared the picnic under the trees. The children returned to the model railway as soon as they'd finished their dessert, leaving Juliet and Sam lying on the picnic rug.

It brought back memories of New Year's Eve when they'd shared a blanket on the beach. When Sam had kissed her. Despite his tireless proposals, he hadn't kissed her properly since that night. He'd been a perfect gentleman and Juliet still didn't know whether she should be relieved or disappointed. In the cold light of day she knew she wasn't ready for anything more than a kiss but at night, alone in her bed, she often imagined how it would feel to be back in Sam's arms, how it would feel to have his comforting bulk wrapped around her.

She fiddled with the bracelet on her wrist—the one Sam had given her on New Year's Eve. Except for when she'd undergone surgery she hadn't taken it off. Sam reached across and put his hand over hers and the warmth from his fingers spread through her like liquid gold. With his other hand he pulled a parcel from the pocket of his jacket.

He handed her the present. 'Happy birthday, Jules.'

The present was small, the size of a jewellery box. Juliet unwrapped the gift, opening the lid to reveal another charm for her bracelet. It was a miniature spray of flowers.

The flowers had silver stems and golden petals.

'Yellow tulips.' Her voice was husky and soft, and her emotions were running high. He hadn't forgotten. Her eyes filled with tears. It was the most beautiful charm she'd ever seen. 'It's gorgeous. Where on earth did you find this?'

'I had it made. Tulips are our thing.' Sam sat up, kneeling on the picnic rug. 'There's something I want to ask you.'

Juliet smiled. 'My answer is still no.' She knew what was coming and part of her recognised she would have been disappointed if Sam hadn't proposed today, but her answer was still the same.

'But why? I know you, Jules. Better than anyone. I know that every year on your birthday you make plans for the year ahead. I want you to include me in those plans. Let's make a fresh start.' He looked directly into her eyes. His green eyes were dark, their colour intense. 'Today is the perfect day to begin again. I love you, Jules, and I want to marry you.' She shook her head but he held up a hand. 'You've finished your chemo treatment, your blood tests are clear, you've had your last surgery, you're running out of reasons to say no. Unless you don't love me?'

He was tracing little circles on her wrist now

with his thumb, sending sparks of desire shooting up her arm. There was no doubt in her mind
that she still loved him. Still wanted him. But
she wasn't going to let her heart rule her head.

She looked back at him, forcing herself to keep
her gaze steady. 'This isn't about me not loving
you, it's about priorities. Our family is my priority but I still don't think we are yours. The navy
is your first love.'

'No. It was, I admit that, but things have
changed. I've changed. Almost losing you has
made me realise how foolish I've been. A job is
nothing compared to my family.'

'But time after time the navy has taken you
away from me and that hasn't changed. I did
think for a while that maybe I'd been unfair,
making you choose between us and the navy. I
thought maybe I should have continued to follow
you wherever you went, but now I'm tired. I could
pretend I'm fine but the truth is I'm exhausted
and I don't want to move. I'm not going to say
it's because of the children. I just don't think I
have the energy any more.'

'I didn't choose the navy over you. I tried the
alternative but I couldn't do it. That job with the

oil company was killing me. I felt like a failure because I couldn't enjoy that job. I was a failure at civilian life and a failure as a father and husband. The navy was what I was good at.'

'You weren't a failure, Sam. You were a fantastic dad, you *are* a fantastic dad. I love you but I can't keep moving. I just can't do it. I'm sorry. I can't marry you.'

'You love me?'

She nodded. 'I always have but I don't think loving you is enough. I can't compete with the sea.'

'Is that your only objection?' he asked. 'What if you didn't have to compete any more? Would you take me back then?'

'There's no point in having this conversation, is there? That's purely hypothetical.'

Sam shook his head. 'What if I told you this job at HMAS *Cerberus* could become permanent?'

'Permanent? A desk job? Are you sure it's the right thing for you?' Juliet had her doubts. She'd seen the fallout of Sam's last attempt at sitting in an office and while she knew he'd been testing the waters for the last five months, that was still a very different proposition from accepting a permanent posting in her mind.

'This is everything a desk job should be. I'm not crunching numbers, doing someone else's mundane tasks. I'm doing practical stuff and it means I can be home with my family. With you. I'm begging you, Jules. Please marry me.'

He reached out and tucked a strand of hair behind her ear and her senses sprang to life. It was her birthday, a day for making decisions.

'Are you going to take this job regardless of my answer?' she asked.

Sam nodded. 'I've already accepted it. I want to be here for you and the children in whatever form you'll have me.'

It was a day for making decisions but was it a day to follow her heart? She took a deep breath. 'I'll think about it.'

Sam's smile lit up his face. 'That's so much better than no!' He jumped up, pulling her to her feet as Puffing Billy blew its whistle. He gathered her in his arms and kissed her, and she nearly changed her mind then and there. Perhaps they could have a future. Perhaps she could do this. Sam's kisses were very persuasive. She couldn't think of any good reason not to spend the rest of her life with him. She couldn't think of anything at all.

And that was why she knew she couldn't give him an answer now. She needed some time and space to get some clarity. She had to think logically.

The children were in bed, exhausted after their big day out. Juliet had just said goodbye to Sam and made herself a cup of tea to take to bed when the phone rang. She had been planning on using the quiet time to work out what she could tell Sam and she debated about whether or not to answer the phone. A quick phone call wouldn't hurt, she decided.

'Happy birthday, Jules.' Maggie's voice came down the line. 'How was your day?'

'Good,' Juliet said with a smile.

'Did Sam propose again?' Maggie was back in Sydney but she knew that Juliet had spent the day with Sam and the kids.

'Yes.'

'He hasn't given up yet?'

'Not yet,' Juliet replied.

'What did you say this time?'

'I said I'd think about it.'

'Really!' Maggie gave an excited squeal. 'I'm not interrupting anything, am I?'

'No. He's gone back to the base. He's got an early start tomorrow, some big training exercise.'

'So tell me what's happened. Why have you changed your answer?'

'Sam is staying in Victoria. He's transferred permanently to *Cerberus*.'

'You're kidding? That's great news. So why didn't you say yes? What are you thinking about?' Maggie peppered Juliet with questions.

'I don't want to make the same mistake twice.'

'What mistake? Marrying him? Sam has done everything you wanted him to. He's obviously committed to your family. Are you? Do you love him?' The questions kept coming.

'Yes.'

'Then I think you'd be making a mistake *not* to marry him. What are you waiting for?'

'I'm scared.'

'Of what?'

'I'm scared of the physical side of things.' Juliet hadn't told Sam that because it hadn't been until he'd stopped kissing her and she'd thought of what would come next that she'd realised what had been holding her back. She knew it was silly, childish even, to worry, and it wasn't Sam's reaction that concerned her. He'd told her everything she needed to hear but she knew from past experience that the reality might be very different. To her at least. And she didn't know if she had enough confidence.

'Why? I thought that was why you decided to go ahead with the reconstructive surgery.'

'That was part of the reason but I haven't tested the waters yet. I still don't know if I'm ready for the whole naked thing.'

'There's only one way to find out. The two of you need a weekend away together.' Maggie loved to organise things and Juliet could tell she sensed a chance to take over. 'Why don't you book something? I'll come down to Melbourne to mind the kids, or you could drop them off with me in Sydney and go to Lilianfels in the Blue Mountains—it doesn't get much more romantic than that. What do you think?'

Juliet knew she'd only be allowed off the phone after she agreed to Maggie's idea. She conceded her idea probably had merit. If she couldn't relax with Sam there was no hope for her, so in the interests of an early night she accepted.

'Okay. I'll look into it, I promise.'

Juliet had dropped the children at school and she was planning on using her free morning to get her new tulip charm attached to her bracelet and then look into a romantic weekend getaway. She would surprise Sam with the trip, she'd decided. It was her turn to do something nice for him. Maggie was right. This weekend would be just what they needed.

She got into the car and nosed out into the traffic just as the nine o'clock news came on. What she heard made her forget all about a romantic getaway. She sat frozen. She'd pulled away from the kerb and the car was sticking into the traffic, blocking the road, but she was completely oblivious to the hold-up she was causing.

'*Repeating our lead story—there has been an explosion on board a navy vessel in Western Port Bay, south of Melbourne.*'

Her heart started racing.

'A navy spokesman has confirmed that at six-twenty this morning there was an unscheduled explosion during a training exercise being run out of HMAS Cerberus.'

Her stomach twisted, tying itself in knots. She took a deep breath, trying to stop herself from gagging. Cars were negotiating their way around her vehicle now, tooting their horns at her as they passed, and she suddenly noticed she was causing a delay. She reversed back into her parking spot as the newsreader continued.

'No fatalities have been reported but two navy personnel were seriously injured and have been airlifted to hospital. Several others have sustained minor injuries and are being treated at the scene.'

Juliet felt physically ill. Sam had gone back to the base last night because he had a two-day training exercise starting today.

She scrambled in her bag for her mobile phone. She hit the button that was the shortcut for Sam's mobile. It went straight to message bank. He was either on the phone or it was switched off. She couldn't bear to think of the third option—that it had been damaged.

She threw the phone onto the passenger seat, checked for traffic, pulled back onto the road and began driving. She wasn't aware of making a conscious decision to head to the base but when she realised she was heading south it seemed as good an option as any and she kept going. She hit the redial button as she drove but the result was the same each time—Sam's message bank.

A round trip took three hours. She had six hours until she had to collect the children. Either she'd reach the base or she'd get through to him on his phone. Either way, she had to speak to him. And she knew what she would say, what she should have said yesterday. Why had she waited? What had she been waiting for?

If the cancer had taught her any lessons, it was that life was short. She hoped she hadn't missed her opportunity. No. She couldn't afford to think like that. Sam would be all right. He had to be. But she wouldn't hesitate again. She was going to get her husband back.

She kept the radio on but there were no further updates.

She kept her phone on but the farther south she got the more concerned she grew. Surely Sam would assume she'd heard the news. If he was all right, why hadn't he rung to tell her? He'd have to know she'd be worried. Why hadn't he called to say everything was okay?

She tried his number again. Nothing.

She was almost there now. She was approaching Hastings. Another ten kilometres to go. Another ten minutes.

An ambulance drove towards her as she exited Hastings. Its lights were flashing but the siren wasn't on. It headed into town, to the hospital, as she continued to drive south.

The gates of HMAS *Cerberus* loomed in front of her. She pulled into the car park on the public side of the gates. She hadn't stopped to think about what she would do once she reached the base. She'd never arrived unannounced before. Sam had always known she was coming.

The gates opened as she neared the sentry post and another ambulance emerged. Juliet watched it pass her by, hoping Sam wasn't inside. Hoping Sam wasn't injured. Or worse.

Traffic was all one way. Coming out. Nothing was going in the other direction.

A small crowd milled around on the outside of the gates. Juliet recognised them for who they were. Navy families, waiting for news. Juliet knew they wouldn't be able to tell her anything. She wondered if anyone could.

Two defence force personnel manned the gate. Both of them looked harassed. Juliet didn't recognise either of them but she figured the sentries were the only defence force personnel she'd be able to talk to as she doubted she'd get into the base.

She approached the sentry post on foot.

'Can I help you, ma'am?' The slightly older-looking sentry addressed her. She obviously wasn't the first person to come looking for information.

'I'm trying to reach my husband, Commander Samuel Taylor? He was supposed to be involved in the training exercise. He's not answering his phone.' Her voice sounded wobbly and she had to make an effort to speak clearly.

'The phone system is jammed, ma'am. Too many calls.' The sentry was holding a clipboard in his hand, and he looked down and wrote something on the paper. 'I'll add his name to the list and if you can wait here, we'll get back to you when we know more.'

She nodded silently, and returned to her car. She'd been hoping for something more definite but this was obviously as much information as she was going to get at this stage. Was that good or bad? Would they have a list of the people who were injured? Would they tell her?

Probably not, she thought. It wasn't in their job description; they were too far down the chain of command. Information like that would come from an officer, a captain or higher, she supposed. She would have to wait. Just like everyone else.

She sat in the driver's seat at ninety degrees to the wheel, leaning her shoulder on the seat, her feet resting outside the car, tapping on the ground. She couldn't sit still; she wasn't good at waiting. Two ambulances had passed her. The radio had said some personnel had been airlifted out. People had been injured. How many? she wondered. Was Sam one of them?

She pulled her phone from her handbag. Her

hands were shaking. Was it worth trying him once more?

An officer, a lieutenant judging by his insignia, exited the base and came to stand in the centre of the car park.

'Ladies and gentlemen, if I could have your attention. The chapel has been made available for those of you who would prefer to wait inside the base. You'll need to undergo security checks but you may be more comfortable waiting in the chapel instead of here. If you'd like to come forward now, we can start the process.'

Still no captain. Who would be coming to give them news?

Most of the people quickly gathered together at the gate, obviously keen to get inside. Juliet joined the queue. They had to show identification and metal detectors were waved over them before they were checked for traces of explosives. Only then were they allowed on base but everyone willingly subjected themselves to the checks. The idea of being on the base instead of waiting outside the gates gave everyone hope. It felt as though they were making progress.

The chapel was an attractive building. It was

built of stone with stained-glass windows, light wooden floors and pews to seat a couple of hundred people. The morning sun was streaming through the eastern windows and the interior of the chapel glowed in the sunlight. Juliet sat alone at the rear of the chapel, unaware of the beauty of her surroundings.

Dust motes kicked up by the throng floated in the air, tiny specks dancing in the currents, coloured pink and gold and green by the light pouring through the stained-glass windows. Juliet noticed the dust and was reminded of a similar scene almost a year earlier when the dust motes had been pale grey. Last July, when she'd been sitting waiting to go before the judge, waiting for her divorce. Now she was waiting again. Waiting to see if the man she'd divorced, the man she loved, was all right. Waiting to see if she was going to get another chance or whether she was too late.

She sat in a pew and stared ahead vacantly. No longer seeing the dust motes. No longer seeing anybody.

How many chances did she deserve? She'd survived the first stage of breast cancer and she'd been resuscitated on an operating table. If Sam was okay, surely that made third time lucky. How many more chances could she expect? This was it. She couldn't wait for life to be perfect—it obviously didn't work like that.

'Jules?'

She turned at the sound of her name. At the sound of his voice.

'Sam!' She sprang from the pew and flung her arms around him. She felt him flinch. She pulled back, just enough to get a look at him, not so far that she had to let go. His blond hair was damp—was it from sweat or water? He had streaks of dirt on his cheek and he looked exhausted, even though it was only late morning. Juliet wasn't used to seeing him look dishevelled when he was in uniform. He was normally immaculate. 'What's wrong? Are you hurt?' She ran her eyes over him, looking for damage. His left arm was tucked close against his side and he had a bandage wrapped around the palm of his left hand. Without thinking, she reached for his arm. 'What happened?' She saw Sam wince as she moved his arm.

'I'm fine,' he said. 'Just bruised ribs and a burn on my hand. It's nothing.'

He didn't look fine.

'Really, I'm okay,' he insisted. 'What are you doing here?'

'I was worried. I heard about the explosion on the radio but I couldn't get through to you,' she explained. 'Next thing I know I was driving this way. I guessed you'd answer my call at some point but before I knew it I was here.'

'You were worried about me?'

'Of course I was. The news said people were injured. I knew you had a training exercise. I thought you'd ring me…'

He pulled her in close with his right arm, holding her tight. His arms were strong and comforting.

'My phone was in my cabin. I couldn't get back there after the explosion.'

'You were on that vessel?' She felt her heart skip a beat and her knees were weak. She wobbled slightly and Sam quickly pulled her into a pew and made her sit.

He nodded. He didn't seem perturbed by what

Juliet could only assume was a near miss. Was he that used to things blowing up around him?

He probably was.

'So what did happen?' Now she was glad she'd driven down here. If she'd heard that he'd been on the ship and hadn't seen for herself that he was okay, she'd be a nervous wreck. More of a nervous wreck, she amended her thoughts.

'We're not sure yet.'

'And the others? I saw ambulances. They said on the radio that people had been airlifted out.' Now that she knew Sam was alive she could afford to think about the others involved, about all those other families waiting to hear something—anything.

'The injuries were relatively minor, thankfully. Some burns and broken bones, a concussion or two but no fatalities. They airlifted a couple of sailors out who had compound leg fractures but they should be fine. It could have been much worse. We've got the details on the injured now, and their families are being informed.'

Juliet looked around the chapel and saw that clusters of people were being spoken to by officers. Information was being imparted.

'What are you going to do now?' Sam asked her.

'I don't know,' she said. She hadn't got to that part of her plan yet. She didn't really have a plan. 'I guess I'll drive back to Melbourne.'

'I'd drive you but I have to go back to work. Things are going to be rather hectic for a few days, I reckon.' He lifted his left hand and brushed his thumb across her cheek. The gauze of the bandage scratched her skin but his thumb was soft. 'Will you be okay?'

'Yes, yes.' He leant forward to kiss her cheek and she knew he was about to stand up and leave. She put one hand on his forearm, stopping him. 'Before you go, there's just one thing I need to ask you.' Sam relaxed into the pew. 'I was going to save this for a more romantic setting but I think I've wasted enough time already.' Very carefully she took Sam's hands and held them in her lap. 'When you proposed yesterday I said I would think about it. And this is what I think.' She took a deep breath and continued. 'I know I've been stubborn and demanding, I know I've been difficult, but I was afraid. I was afraid of coming second again, of always competing for time and attention with your career. And I was afraid of intimacy. Not emotionally but physically. But I decided last night that I had to get past that but then, this morning, when I couldn't reach you on the phone, that's when I knew what fear really was. I've coped with a lot of things over the past year but I didn't know how I would cope if something had happened to you. I realised I've been worrying about things that don't matter. Thinking I had all the time in the world when I should have known better. I've wasted enough time.' Sam was watching her, his green eyes intense. She could tell he knew what she was about to say. He smiled and that was all the encouragement she needed to continue. 'I love you and, if you'll still have me, I will marry you.'

His smile grew wider, the left side of his mouth caught up to the right and his eyes shone. He pulled his hands free and hugged her again, hugged her hard. 'Of course I'll still have you. We're meant to be together.'

'Scars and all?' she asked as he released her.

'Scars and all.' He ran one hand up her side, sliding it under her shirt, stopping at the bottom of her ribs. Juliet gasped as a surge of desire shot through her. Sam was still smiling as he slid his hand around her back and pulled her close. 'However you come is fine with me, you know that. And put back together is better than not having you at all. Your scars will remind us of what is important, of where we've come from. I love you more than you can imagine and that has never changed.'

'You're sure?'

'I've never been more certain of anything in my life. I chose you fourteen years ago and I choose you again today and I will choose you again tomorrow. We have a lifetime ahead of us. I just wish it could start right now.'

So did she, but even Juliet knew that sometimes she just had to be patient. 'It's okay. I actually do understand that work comes first in this case. I can wait.' She smiled. 'Not for ever, mind you, but for a little longer. We will have the rest of our lives to make up for tonight, won't we?'

'We most certainly will, my love, we most certainly will.' His smile spread slowly this time, full of promises, teasing, enticing, and her smile matched his. Slowly, so slowly, he bent his head to hers, joining them together with a kiss, sealing his promise to her with tenderness. Juliet kissed him back, using her lips to send him a message of love, trust and hope. She could feel her spirit responding to Sam's touch, her body and soul growing warmer with every passing second as the heat spread from her lips to her heart and rushed through the core of her, swamping the adrenaline that her fear had unleashed.

Juliet shook as she realised how close she'd come to losing everything. She could feel Sam rubbing her back to keep her warm but it wasn't the temperature that was making her shiver. The adrenaline was wearing off now that the danger had passed. The fear had gone but she was still tense and jittery.

Sam broke the kiss. He was watching her, his green eyes dark and intense, and she imagined she could see through them like windows to his soul.

'I love you, Jules. You are everything to me.' His eyes lightened in colour as he spoke and she could almost see his love for her pouring out from their emerald depths. 'When I can get away from here we are going shopping for an engagement ring. I want to make this official. I've waited long enough.'

'I don't need a new ring,' she protested.

'You don't?'

'No.' She slid her old engagement ring from her right hand and gave it to Sam. 'I don't even need a new husband.'

Sam was frowning now, looking puzzled. 'But—'

'My old husband was perfect for me,' she explained. 'I just didn't see enough of him. If I can have him back, I'll be happy.' She held her left hand out, fingers spread, waiting for Sam.

'Are you sure?' he asked.

'Positive,' she replied. 'I love you. All I ever wanted was to be with you.'

Sam held the ring between his right thumb and forefinger and slid it onto Juliet's left hand. 'You will be, I promise. I am yours, now and for ever,' he said.

Juliet looked at her hand, at where her finger was encircled by the gold band. The ring signalled their promise to each other. They had come full circle and she was back where she belonged. She had her husband back. Her family was complete. Her world was perfect.

'We made it.'

'Yes, we did,' Sam agreed as he bent his head to kiss her once more. 'Yes, we did.'

MEDICAL™

Large Print

Titles for the next six months...

August

CEDAR BLUFF'S MOST ELIGIBLE BACHELOR	Laura Iding
DOCTOR: DIAMOND IN THE ROUGH	Lucy Clark
BECOMING DR BELLINI'S BRIDE	Joanna Neil
MIDWIFE, MOTHER...ITALIAN'S WIFE	Fiona McArthur
ST PIRAN'S: DAREDEVIL, DOCTOR...DAD!	Anne Fraser
SINGLE DAD'S TRIPLE TROUBLE	Fiona Lowe

September

SUMMER SEASIDE WEDDING	Abigail Gordon
REUNITED: A MIRACLE MARRIAGE	Judy Campbell
THE MAN WITH THE LOCKED AWAY HEART	Melanie Milburne
SOCIALITE...OR NURSE IN A MILLION?	Molly Evans
ST PIRAN'S: THE BROODING HEART SURGEON	Alison Roberts
PLAYBOY DOCTOR TO DOTING DAD	Sue MacKay

October

TAMING DR TEMPEST	Meredith Webber
THE DOCTOR AND THE DEBUTANTE	Anne Fraser
THE HONOURABLE MAVERICK	Alison Roberts
THE UNSUNG HERO	Alison Roberts
ST PIRAN'S: THE FIREMAN AND NURSE LOVEDAY	Kate Hardy
FROM BROODING BOSS TO ADORING DAD	Dianne Drake

MILLS & BOON

MEDICAL™

Large Print

November

HER LITTLE SECRET	Carol Marinelli
THE DOCTOR'S DAMSEL IN DISTRESS	Janice Lynn
THE TAMING OF DR ALEX DRAYCOTT	Joanna Neil
THE MAN BEHIND THE BADGE	Sharon Archer
ST PIRAN'S: TINY MIRACLE TWINS	Maggie Kingsley
MAVERICK IN THE ER	Jessica Matthews

December

FLIRTING WITH THE SOCIETY DOCTOR	Janice Lynn
WHEN ONE NIGHT ISN'T ENOUGH	Wendy S. Marcus
MELTING THE ARGENTINE DOCTOR'S HEART	Meredith Webber
SMALL TOWN MARRIAGE MIRACLE	Jennifer Taylor
ST PIRAN'S: PRINCE ON THE CHILDREN'S WARD	Sarah Morgan
HARRY ST CLAIR: ROGUE OR DOCTOR?	Fiona McArthur

January

THE PLAYBOY OF HARLEY STREET	Anne Fraser
DOCTOR ON THE RED CARPET	Anne Fraser
JUST ONE LAST NIGHT…	Amy Andrews
SUDDENLY SINGLE SOPHIE	Leonie Knight
THE DOCTOR & THE RUNAWAY HEIRESS	Marion Lennox
THE SURGEON SHE NEVER FORGOT	Melanie Milburne

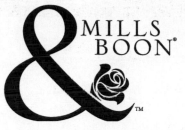